The Ordinary Lives of Others

SCOTT MILLIN

To Dad:
Who has given so much to the lives of others.

CONTENTS

Educated in a small town
Taught the fear of Jesus in a small town
Used to daydream in that small town
Another boring romantic that's me

John Mellencamp

THE PLACE THAT I CALLED HOME

When I moved into town it made the paper. *The Minuteman Post* printed it on page seven under the Other Local News section, with the headline, "*Minister, Family Moving into Church Parsonage Shortly.*" The article went on to list my father's educational background and previous job experience, and the five paragraph story ended with, "*The family has three children.*"

It was not exactly a Hollywood headline, but on a frigid January evening in 1970, Dad became the new minister in town, making my family a little more newsworthy in this small New England community. While the story was written before we arrived in town, it was not published until the day after we had unpacked our belongings and settled into our new home. News travels fast but not always in a small-town newspaper.

My hometown is a narrow strip of land located in the northeast corner of the state, where the tips of the Atlantic's watery fingers extend inland from The Sound and drain into marshland and tide pools. Like so many other New England communities, Main Street snakes through farmland and forest and serves as the primary passage to anyplace else.

In my youth, the town center was elongated over a continuous half-mile stretch of Main Street, beginning with the unimpressive but prevalent town common. The central green played host to youth baseball games, a week-long summer carnival, and family cook-outs and picnics. The common was followed by a yellow timbered town hall, a lonely brick savings bank, and a few sleepy shops and markets. Shortly thereafter sat a simple wooden structure that housed the odd-couple tenants of Harland's Hardware Store and Doctor Bartlett's office. Commerce was conducted in all of these places - commerce of necessity, not luxury.

Finally, just after the town's only traffic light, the center ended with a sprawling wrought iron fenced-in cemetery and adjoining white clapboard Congregational Church - my father's new place of work. The church served as the primary place of worship for the residents, and its towering and pointed steeple had a deep green clock face with crisp white roman numerals and arrows for hands. The copper and bronze cast bell lay hidden behind louvered shutters but could be heard ringing every hour and just prior to each Sunday morning service.

If you grew up in New England, I may have described a place that sounds a lot like your hometown. Perhaps it is.

New Englanders are a hardy breed, and their roots are deep and grow out of the same soil as the settlers who once laid claim to this land. The 1600's saw a great migration to what is now New England. Waves of Puritans, religious rebels, relocated to the new world to build their own shining "City upon a Hill," an ideal and utopic place where people could worship and live by a different set of rules. Surnames like Bradford,

Bailey, and Turner left England and landed in places just like my hometown. In some cases, these stubborn Protestant bloodlines persevered and remain. I talk about religion – the Protestant kind – not because I am an expert or real enthusiast, but because it serves as the foundation of my hometown and my upbringing.

In blasphemous terms, Protestants are "lazy Catholics." We do not exert ourselves getting down on a bench to pray and do not require children to give up a weekday afternoon to attend church school.

In more appropriate and accurate terms, the Protestants left England for the new world to escape and purify the Church of England. They placed less importance on the men who claimed to speak for God and did away with the pomp, symbolism, and ceremony that permeated the Church. The Puritans believed each individual was beholden to God, and they set out to simplify the way they worshiped and lived.

For the record, Protestants certainly were not – and are not - lazy. One colonial family's diary describes the heart of an early settler quite succinctly: "A colonist seldom made his way to New England unless he were a man of more than usual energy; and he seldom stayed unless he was a man of unusual stubbornness."[1]

Protestants literally shaped the new world, and town lines were not defined by mile markers or hard boundaries as they are now. They were designated by patterns of population that centered around common areas and public buildings - most notably the meeting house (church). One historian wrote that faith was so important to the New England settlers that meeting houses were built within six miles of each other, so "that no person had to walk more than three miles to church." [2]

As a boy, the church lay directly at the end of my driveway but I hardly viewed its close proximity as an advantage.

My particular hometown was established in 1642, by its founding father, the Reverend James P. King - a fact that as students at Whispering Pines Elementary School we studied and learned all about. The Reverend King was a local hero and the best known dead or alive guy in town; he is buried in the town cemetery under an indistinct, leaning headstone (even the Puritans' graves were simple). The Reverend King and his band of nineteen families crossed the ocean, struggled to find food, and faced adversity on a massive scale - the odds were completely against them. Something had to bind these people together if they were to survive, and it was their faith that did it. Faith gave them hope and resolve, and ultimately defined the way they would go on to live - simply, thankfully, and with a quiet sense of purpose. The traits of these settlers passed on through generations and very much described the residents who lived there at the time I arrived.

I always thought that having a 20th Century version of the Reverend King for a father was a pretty cool thing. Dad and I would walk to run errands (Dad and his lanky frame walked with casual purpose while I ran to keep up with his long strides), and each time I witnessed a familiar exchange with the people we passed along the way.

"Hi Reverend. How are you?"

Dad would reply with a sincere smile and head nod,

"Goodandyou?" As a young boy, I used to think that "Goodandyou" was a single word that served as both an answer and a question.

My Dad was not a fire and brimstone preacher who led the good citizens with charges of policy and morality, as Reverend King must have been. Dad did not hand down the word of God or claim to have all the answers. But like his long-gone predecessor, Dad was an important person and was looked upon as a leader in the community. I was proud to be his son.

Dad rolled up his sleeves and walked among the people he served and dealt with his congregation (all people) on a human level. He helped them embrace the goodness and struggle with the darkness that life inevitably brings our way. Dad was one of the few in town who worked on Sundays, but I think his most meaningful acts were performed in the living room and at the kitchen table; by the graveside and in the funeral home; and at the hospital bed-side and waiting room. Sometimes it was performed on an unscheduled basis, in a parking lot or on our doorstep. Dad rarely had a day or a moment off when it came to tending to the needs of others.

Dad seemed to have an understanding of things that most of us never think about until it is too late. It has been told to me by many that Dad was the most important person at a most wonderful or most terrible time in their lives. It was not uncommon after a fire truck or police car went screaming through the center of town for our phone to ring, and the caller to ask if "The Reverend" was available to give counsel and comfort. Since misfortune does not have a set schedule or provide a babysitter, I would sometimes go along with him, and by doing so I bore witness to his acts.

I saw Dad pray with parents whose son ran away after burning down the family barn, and I sat on a front porch while he comforted a family after receiving news their loved one was dying. I kept myself busy with my Matchbox cars as Dad kept the residents of the Glenview Nursing Home busy with communion, conversation, and companionship.

As we sat around our own supper table we listened to Dad recount the events of his day - visits with a family who lost a child, and with men who experienced the brotherhood and horrors of war; conversations with alcoholics, and with families who lost sons to prison. Often the issues were smaller, but Dad dealt with each person the same. He listened and reassured. Dad never judged or condemned.

Nor did he prioritize a person's struggles according to wealth, status, or familiarity. In my father's eyes, everybody was equal and everybody was somebody. Dad practiced what he preached, and he helped the people of my town with something no other public official or leader in town could - their relationship with God.

This was the environment of the town and the household in which I was raised.

The childhood of the son of a minister is a unique existence. I remember playing a weekend game of football with friends on my front lawn and the game came to a screeching halt when a hearse pulled into the driveway. My friends stood and stared, and while none of them said it, I knew they all were thinking the same thing, "There's a dead guy in there!"

Instead, Dad's very much alive, six foot-two inch frame unfolded itself from the front passenger seat and said, "Thanks for the ride, Dave." Dave Emerson was the local funeral home director, and he had given my father a lift home upon the completion of a graveside service. Turning his attention toward me and my open-mouthed friends, Dad gave us a wave and said, "Hi kids!" For Dad, death was another day at the office. But for my friends, football took a back seat, and the next few minutes were spent talking about dead people and wondering what is like to die and how creepy it must be to ride in a car with a corpse.

There are positives and negatives that come with being the son of a preacher.

One of the cons is the expectation that I would follow in my father's footsteps. Other than the time I was asked by my third grade teacher to play the Reverend James P. King in Whispering Pines' Thanksgiving play that vocation never came to pass for me. Growing up with a congregation as my extended (and at times dysfunctional) family was enough for me. In my mind, there was no need to perpetuate such an existence. Besides, that pesky "God-thing" would have become an issue eventually.

Another negative about being the son of a preacher-man in a small Protestant town is that I was very much under the public microscope - anonymity was not an option. If I did a dirty deed it would not be long before I was identified as the culprit. The role also came with expectations, and I was held to a higher standard by the general public when an infraction was committed ("You of all people should know that what you did was wrong!"). But so long as I kept my nose relatively clean, the pros outweighed the cons.

Generally, people assumed I was "God fearing" and wholesome, and I discovered I could take advantage of those expectations - or at least ride the wave of undeserved, assumptive goodwill cast my way. I was slightly mischievous, but in no way was I a wolf in sheep's clothing...despite being accused by my sisters of, "getting away with murder all the time." I simply prefer to think of it as clever marketing on my part.

I found that if I behaved myself and dressed well enough, the townspeople gave me credit for being a good boy and more trustworthy than the kid who sat a few pews down from me. Therefore, I was usually given the benefit of the doubt, rarely looked upon with suspicion (even when I should have been), and allowed access to places, situations, and conversations that other boys my age might have been shooed away from.

Otherwise, I did all the normal things a normal boy does. I played Little League baseball, rode my bike to the ends of the earth, swam in the estuary at the town landing, suffered through band and chorus, and played King of the Hill on a dirt pile to test my mettle. These were just some of the definable, unforgettable moments and experiences.

Reverend King and his faithful Puritan flock sought a better way of life, and as I reflect back on my childhood, life certainly *seemed* simpler and purer than it does today. We played outside until the street lights came on; organized our own games and activities; had supper together at the table; believed that good enough was good enough; and did not make politics so personal. In the 1970's, there was mischief in the young, but it was still partially swathed in a fraying blanket of innocence.

Certainly my New England hometown was not the New World utopia the Puritans had set out to create, but I think there are many of us who look back on our childhood and feel as if they came pretty close. However, as those of us who have grown up and grown old eventually find out, nothing lasts forever. There came a time when I had to leave my childhood and my hometown behind.

I often return and walk the side streets and the hallways of Whispering Pines Elementary. I sit in the pews of my father's church and I stand among the reeds of the great saltmarsh. I gaze upon the buildings and the landmarks that surrounded me as a boy and I seek the people and feel the energy of those who lived and died there. I return because it gives me a feeling of familiarity and belonging - it takes me home.

Please do not misunderstand me. I do not physically return to my hometown. Seventeen has turned forty-something in the blink of an eye, and I am now an unknown to the people who reside there today. While there might be many who recall my father and my family, time has inserted itself between us and made us strangers. Nor do I wish to view what has become of the pastures and farmlands that once lined Main Street, or take in the sight of a shuttered and boarded up Harland's Hardware. Going home again would only bring me disappointment. My time there has come and gone. The people and places of my hometown are just memories for me now.

Instead, I return to my hometown using my mind's eye and the recollections that are embedded in my brain and played in a constant loop. It is easy for me to do as the experiences of my youth lie just beneath the surface of who I am today.

I am not an educated man when it comes to the human condition. I possess no fancy title or degree. But I can tell you that when I write about the people and events of my hometown it brings me comfort. When I write about the scenery and the landmarks that surrounded me as a boy it puts my troubles as a grown man at ease. In my time and in my head I have accumulated a multitude of stories about the people and the places of my hometown. Now is the time for me to get them out - not to erase or forget them, but to release them.

The people of my small New England hometown led ordinary lives, and within their ordinary lives there were extraordinary moments in time witnessed and retained by the son of a minister. These are the stories of the people who lived in a place that I called home.

I wrote them to share them with you, but also to save myself.

LEARNING TO FLY, '70

On a suffocatingly hot day, smack in the middle of August, a boy travelled in the back seat of his family's car. It was the kind of day that you remember when you think back about a summer day from your own childhood.

The air smelled an earthy mix of fresh cut grass and wildflowers, and the sun sat high in the sky, causing the buildings to splash shadows across the sidewalks on both sides of Main Street. In the background, the steamy buzz of the cicadas told you what you already knew.

The boy's bare legs were sweaty and sticky on the fabric of the seat. He was restless. The window was open but the stream of warm air provided little relief. The boy's arm lay draped over the edge of the aluminum molding that housed the opened window frame, and his sweaty forehead leaned on his shoulder. Out of boredom, his eyes focused on his hand as it dangled out the window.

He remembered that his dad had once told him how an airplane was able to fly, and that his small hand was no different than the wing on the massive steel birds that flew so high above them.

His dad, who liked to understand things that others could not, said the hand spliced the air in half, and that because of the way the hand was cupped, the wind going above moved faster than the wind moving below. The differences in airspeed created differences in pressure above and below his hand, which created "lift."

The boy stretched his palm face down, cupped his hand, and held his fingers tight together. If he tried real hard he could find the right balance - the point where his arched hand sliced through the humid air with the least amount of resistance, and floated - free of gravity's pull and free from the push of the headwind created by the motion of the car. But as soon as he found that point, he lost it. So the boy struggled to find it again. When he did, he struggled to hold it there.

Balance, in all things, can be difficult to find and maintain.

The boy craned his neck out of the car window, causing the roaring wind to slap him in the face and blow his bangs up wildly. He squinted into the onrushing air as it thundered in his ears, and he watched a small, silvery jet set against a clear blue sky.

Just the simple act of leaning out further into the maelstrom of air currents was enough to throw off the balance of his hand. It bounced up and down like an out of control kite, and if it were not attached at his wrist, his hand would have crashed down onto the pavement and bounced its way to a lonely stop, like an empty soda can tossed from a speeding vehicle.

The boy pulled his head back inside the window and he worked to find the balance point again, thinking all the while of how one slight twitch and his "wing" went out of control. He wondered how something as giant as an airplane could be subject to the same principles as his own fleshy little hand.

His father's words about the symmetry between these two incongruous things now seemed dubious, at best. Was it lift, or was it something else? Without proof, what was he to believe?

The boy and his family were riding in a 1966, green Volkswagen Squareback. There is no need to describe the vehicle's features any further because its name is also its definition.

His parents bought this car because they were practical people. The American automobile industry was in the throes of young adulthood, and testosterone and ego lay behind the design and purchase of most cars on the road at that time. The stout Chevy Camaro, the mean Dodge Charger, and the bullet shaped Pontiac Trans Am - with its sleek lines, shiny paint job, and Bird of Fire emblem - were just a few of the lean and mean American muscle cars that laid patches of rubber on a nationwide sea of sand and gravel. The late 1960's and early '70's were the time of the great American Automobile Allure - to everyone, so it seemed, but the boy's parents.

They liked the idea of being different from

everybody else - of quietly putting around at their own pace while the rest of the world roared by in a hurry. The boy's parents cared little of what others thought, and more often than not, believed that different was better.

Foreign cars were few, and the German Squareback was an oddity. His family's car was one of a kind in their small but busy coastal town. But that gave the boy's parents a sense of pride, and it fulfilled their need for function over form.

The family car, while not the preferred means of transportation for the boy, provided him with an escape from life as he knew it - a chance to see how other people lived their daily lives, and to observe the makeup of their surroundings. It mattered little where he went, so long as he went somewhere – the town dump swarming with the stench of things people no longer wanted, the grocery store with the "smiley lady" who punched prices into the cash register with her stubby fingers, or a trip to the beach after supper when the sun set and night washed itself over the land. These were all places with new people to watch and new experiences to experience.

Sometimes the boy would sit in the Squareback as it sat idle in the driveway. He would pretend that he was driving to someplace he'd never been, depressing the clutch and shifting its manual transmission into each gear. He hummed to simulate the noise the engine would make, rising in volume and pitch before shifting into the next, higher gear. He tried to mimic everything his parents did, including proper use of the car's directional and hand over hand pattern when turning the black, leather-wrapped steering wheel.

The mechanics of his family car - of all cars - mystified him. When he glanced around at the myriad of lights, buttons, and knobs he wondered how so many small pieces and moving parts were imagined, created, and assembled. It seemed as if, all around him, new things were constantly being made, progress was happening, and people were moving forward with certainty, direction, and self-assuredness.

The boy watched the world race by, like one of those muscle cars he admired and he watched the others keep pace. He feared that he would not be able to roar toward his own destiny and would continue to sputter through his own life, like the Squareback on a Sunday drive.

Fear can be an awful thing. For some it can motivate and move them forward, but for others it can cripple and calcify.

Like his hand that hung out of the car window he searched for his own balance, and as he propelled through life he was continuously caught between the forces that pushed at him - opportunity and risk, and the forces that pulled on him - self-doubt and insecurity.

He was barely aloft and he worked hard to find his trajectory, sense of purpose, and lift.

A TALE OF TWO JOES, '71

Joe was sitting in someone else's chair, in someone else's room. The sealed up window in front of him let in a soft yellow beam of sunlight, and the rectangular heater that sat alongside the wall pumped out a steady current of warm air.

Joe's chair faced the window, and next to him sat an empty one - both seats were angled as if someone had arranged them so that the sitter was forced to dwell on the events going on outside, rather than inside the room. Behind Joe were two beds with matching nightstands.

Joe was aware enough to know that he was stuck in this familiar strange place again. It caused him troubles, and he wrung his hands together as if he were trying to wash away whatever it was that troubled him. Joe stared out the window at the trees blowing in the wind.

The window pane was thick and it muffled all sound - Joe was on the inside looking out. He liked the way the trees swung silently back and forth, and the way their green leaves danced and turned inside out with each gust, revealing a slightly different and duller shade on their undersides. All the while, the trees' sturdy trunks and full branches alternated leaning left and right at a steady and rhythmic pace. Without realizing it, their gentle dance helped ease his troubles.

He and Ethel finished digging just before twilight. They heaved the last bucket-full of dirt with a pulley and rope, and as he dumped its contents into the wooden wheelbarrow he imagined what their house would look like when it was all finished.

The maple trees loomed large around him, and they were counting on them to grow even larger to cover their house with shade from the summer sun. He lifted and turned the wheelbarrow, and huffed it down to the bottom of their property line and dumped its contents. This will make good soil for the garden, he thought.

Ethel smiled, tightened the handkerchief that covered her hair, and wiped the sweat from her brow with her sleeve. She had faith in him, and together they would build their house.

Joe felt the urge to move. His mind told him it was time to go home and to sit in his own chair. So he pushed himself up and went to find his way home.

He eased open the door to his room and glanced around, peering down the long hallway. Nobody seemed to take notice of him and all the faces meant nothing to him. He did not know where he was but he knew where he wanted to be – home. The feeling was instinctual, not reasoned, and as he took his first step into the hallway, Joe noticed the thin slippers that covered his feet. He wondered how they got there.

They ordered their house from a Sears and Roebuck mail order catalogue. He and Ethel chose The Milford Model, item # 3385, as shown on page twenty seven, and it cost them $1,671. They liked the lines and layout and agreed with the description under the picture that read, "A home like the Milford is a credit to you, your family, and every neighborhood." When the lumber arrived by train it was pre-cut and fitted and needed only to be assembled by a craftsman. So, together he and Ethel finished building their house.

Joe made it down the hallway and pushed the door

open that led to a stairwell, which he hoped led to home. As the door slipped open a loud bell sounded. The noise startled him so much that, going against his own desires, he stepped back. They came running in their white uniforms, grabbed him by his hand and led him away, further away from the door and further from home.

They made false promises and played tricks with his head. They seemed intent on confusing him into submission: You have guests coming and they'll want you to be here when they visit. We don't have a car for you to leave in right now. Don't worry, your tomato plants are being taken care of.

Joe's eyes were a cloudy blue and betrayed the confusion that lay behind them. On his wrist was a silver and gold Timex watch with a flex-band. As they guided him back to his room and sat him down in front of the window, he glanced at his watch and wondered if it was keeping proper time. He feared that perhaps it had slowed down a minute or two. Joe slid the band off his wrist and turned it over so that the smooth silver backing faced him. *I'd better fix it*, he thought.

He worked with his hands and his mind, depending equally on each to get the job done. He was a clockmaker, and he worked out back in his shop with his tools, while Ethel worked out front in the store with their customers. He made clocks of all kinds, crafting their cases out of pine, maple, and oak. The sawdust coated his workshop floor and was always in his hair and in the wrinkles and creases of his skin. He assembled the clocks' gears, chains, weights, and pendulums, and perfected their timing with fussy precision. He enjoyed making mantle clocks and wall clocks, but his specialty and true passion was the long case - the Grandfather clock.

Joe sat slumped at a round table in a room with lots of other round tables. There were six chairs circling his and he ate his supper with two other men he did not know, one of whom was sound asleep with his head hanging over his plate. A television could be heard blaring from the next room and it almost covered up the sound of the clinking silverware. Eating was merely an exercise. He swirled his spoon around in his mashed potatoes and creamed corn. Joe felt nothing.

His garden was green and lush. Squash and zucchini burst

from the vine, and cucumbers grew as much as two inches in a single, humid summer day. The tomatoes were plump and red and he loved to eat them like an apple, letting the juice run down his arm.

Ethel picked the lettuce daily and pickled the beets, beans, and peppers. His stalks of corn were always knee high by the 4th of July, and a proud seven feet tall by August. The only thing he loved more than growing his corn was eating it, savoring the butter and salt mixture, and wearing the juicy spray of the yellow and white kernels on his clothes and chin. Ethel cooked the freshly picked ears in her large, black and white speckled Graniteware bucket, over the outdoor fire pit. He was convinced that is what made it taste so good.

Joe was frequently visited by strangers and they sat alongside him in his room, taking their place in the empty chair next to his. They talked about the weather, told him about their day, and made small-talk between long pauses of silence. When Joe felt like talking he would nod his head and state empty questions like, "Is that right," or, "How about that."

One stranger came more often than most, and Joe liked her and enjoyed her company. She was the one who was most like him, and she seemed to understand him, even though he did not understand himself. She made things better and more familiar than they seemed when she was not there – and that made him happy.

They felt lucky to have such fine girls. There was a hammock that stretched between two trees in the backyard, and that was his favorite place to sit with them and share some vanilla ice cream - just he and his two chums with a bowl and three spoons, cuddled up together and rocking back and forth as the sun set on their day.

Joe had no sense of time. Each day ticked away, and he was unaware of its passing and of his place within it. Each day was the same as the one before, yet each day was different and unfamiliar – he was in an undeserved purgatory. Joe was like an aged Grandfather clock whose uniquely crafted frame was worn and seasoned to a natural antique perfection but whose internal workings misfired and were unable to measure or keep time with any accuracy. Joe's memory was caught in a foggy, faulty loop of confusion. He was betrayed by the very mind that served him so well for so long.

Each night, after supper was finished and the dishes and homework were done, they sat in the den of the house he and Ethel built.

Their two chairs were side by side and angled towards one another, purposely arranged so that the focus was the center of the room and everything that happened in and around it. They sat together and talked about the memories made and experiences shared. They did this for over forty years, and after Ethel died he still sat there, alone – reliving those memories, cherishing, and relying on them.

His brain replayed all that his senses had captured over the course of their life together: The smell of the turkey roasting in the oven on Thanksgiving; the crackle of the fire from behind the iron curtain of the brick fireplace; the smell of Ivory soap in the bathroom; the creak of the black leather recliner, followed by the shuffling of newspapers; the roughness of the girls' tiny footprints, preserved in the concrete base of the flagpole; and the sound of the coo-coo clock's call at the passing hour.

He had a good life, and he was grateful for the memories he had. He took comfort in knowing that he would always have them.

FURTHER ON UP THE ROAD, '72

Little Jennifer was the youngest of five Gables children, all of whom were well kept and well-mannered. But there was something special (almost perfect) about Little Jennifer. She was grace and beauty combined, and what made her even more beautiful was that she was completely unaware of it.

Her skin was fair and flush with life in the winter and bronzed smartly by the sun in the summer. Even her fingers and toes (prone to those pesky imperfections) were graced by beauty - Dr. Scholl's and a mood ring were obscurers, not enhancers. Her hair was long and golden and always garnished with a ribbon or flower. Her voice was strong and pure, prompting the church choir director to tell Mrs. Gables that, "Little Jennifer has the voice of an angel."

Little Jennifer's brothers never laid a finger on their sister and they were always there to look out for her in the school yard. Mind you, there was nothing about her that anyone disliked or held in contempt - it was just the silly boys who tried to draw her attention who sometimes caused a nuisance.

Small towns leave little room for obscurity, and the people in this small town all saw Little Jennifer grow and blossom into a young woman. The people in town liked her.

As with most girls at a young age, Little Jennifer played dolls and dress-up and dreamed of the day she would have children of her own. She hosted make-believe tea parties, performed plays in the backyard with her friends, and every summer (even as a teenager) she set up a lemonade stand in her front yard – a simple card table with a carefully constructed cardboard sign that read, "Thirsty? Let My Lemon-ADE You!" Under those words was a lemon, with a smiley face.

The Gables' house sat across the street from the town common, which served as the home for the town's Little League baseball games, the summer carnival, and the conclusion of the 4th of July parade.

All of these events sent plenty of thirsty customers Little Jennifer's way, and during the spring and summer months she deposited her modest profits in her savings account at the bank.

After Little Jennifer deposited her money, and during other moments when Mrs. Gables saw her children demonstrate a sense of planning or preparing for what was next in their lives, she would kiss them on the forehead and say, "Dream baby, dream. I believe in you!" Mrs. Gables was an awkward six feet tall and her skin was splotchy from a condition. When she stood, she often placed both of her hands on the back of her hips and pointed her feet off to each side. Little Jennifer did not inherit any of her mother's features or mannerisms, but she radiated the same goodness.

As a high school student, Little Jennifer was planning and saving for the future, and as a young adult she was right on the cusp of realizing those dreams.

One afternoon in late November, Little Jennifer sat at the window of her bright yellow school bus as it made its way back from the outskirts of town. The bus' gears ground their way up and down the scale, and an exhaust of screaming teenagers trailed behind it. The frames of the young adults on board mirrored the contour of the streets below, and they bounced and rattled along in their seats in concert. Little Jennifer sat quiet and composed – surrounded by chaos, but happy in her place.

Her long denim skirt flowed loosely and button-up beige sweater clung tight. Her blonde hair funneled through a sunflower clip at the crest of her head and flowed down and over her shoulders - like a golden waterfall. Little Jennifer sat up straight and gazed out the window, watching the world go by but patiently and confidently waiting for her chance to join it. She failed to notice the boys who snuck a glance in her direction. For them, a quick look at Little Jennifer with the chance of being caught was better than having no glance at all.

The bus made a turn onto Main Street and approached the town common. The common was at the center of town and was intersected and surrounded by streets with names you would expect from a community born before the American Revolution: Independence, Church, Maple, and Main.

The mighty oaks that lined the common's edge clung tight to a few wrinkled hanger-ons, and the skeleton-like branches of the few interior maples revealed that they had long since surrendered theirs. It was the dead of autumn.

There were a variety of buildings that surrounded the common - the savings bank, Emerson's Funeral Home, Dr. Bartlett's office, and the town hall. These were the places where lives merged and crossed. The common was the life of the community, and it was also the neighborhood that Little Jennifer's family called home.

At the near end of the common lay an oversized statue honoring those who died fighting for their country. The tall marker had a glassy reflection of smoked gray and was planted smartly alongside a rusting white flag-pole and a deep green, wooden Little League backstop.

The statue's base had four rectangular sides that

stretched high, and at the top of each quadrant the word Remember, Fallen, Reverence, and Eternal was artfully chiseled. Under each word were the names of those who had perished - over there and over here.

Adorning the statue's base was a solitary, larger than life Union soldier, laden with gear and leaning on his rifle. As the bus passed it by, Little Jennifer noted to herself that his expression and stance revealed the sadness and exhaustion of a soul and nation at war.

Riding along, Little Jennifer recalled how the monument served as the ending spot for the town's 4th of July parade and how the veterans who gathered to drink and tell war stories each and every Friday night at the V.F.W. club served as the color guard. They semi-circled around the flagpole with bellies bulging, flags unfurled, and rifles in hand, and when they fired their guns into the air in a salute it shattered the stillness of the summer air - and any illusions of romance Little Jennifer might have had about war.

She tensed in her seat at the vivid memory of the metallic clicks of the cartridges slamming into their chambers, followed by the indecipherable barking of orders and atomic crack of the rifles. She wondered if her older brother jumped when he fired his rifle, over there.

Reverend Rogers followed the salute with a prayer and scripture quote. He reminded the people that during war-time both the nation and the soldier suffer, and that the sacrifices made for liberty and freedom should not be wrapped into a self-promoting cause or catch-phrase by citizens. A soldier's actions and deeds were to be honored, mourned, and appreciated, and a separate quest for peace endeavored. The Reverend also reassured the good citizens not to fear - that the lost children of war (that all lost children) were welcomed into the Kingdom of Heaven, where they would live forever.

Little Jennifer remembered how the Reverend's words lingered with the rifle smoke over the heads of the crowd, and when he paused for effect there was a heavy silence, disturbed only by an occasional clearing of a throat or a sniffle.

Following the prayer was a moment of silence, at which time the citizens of this good town were given the opportunity to think about (or not) the sacrifices that were made on their behalf. Mrs. Gables would lean down and whisper in her children's ears, instructing them to say a prayer of their own. "All of your prayers will rise up into the heavens, where they will be felt by the departed," she would tell them. Mrs. Gables was absolutely certain of that.

Sitting on the bus as it passed this special gathering place, Little Jennifer closed her eyes and silently mouthed, "You're gone, but I will never forget you." She hoped that the dead would sense her prayer, as her mom suggested.

The whine of the bus' tires changed pitch as it began to decelerate, and Little Jennifer grabbed her pile of books from the seat beside her and placed them on her lap. She slid over and stood up in the center aisle, balancing her delicate body with her perfect little fingers on the rows of seats as she made her way towards the front. The bus came to a deliberate stop, and Little Jennifer Gables gracefully pulled back her shoulders to fight the pull of inertia.

The boys on the bus took notice, and the driver

opened the door with a greasy squeak. Little Jennifer stepped down onto the sidewalk of Main Street, turned, and headed home. The cool autumn air gusted, but the waning afternoon sun wrapped around her, like a blanket.

Jimmy Tompkins caught sight of her figure as he merged his Peterbilt cement mixer onto Main Street, and as he drew closer he leaned forward with anticipation, shifting anxiously up to speed. Jimmy's truck was massive and loud, and caked with dried concrete and dust. The fully loaded, rotating mixer drum brought its weight to sixty-thousand pounds, and the hose that dangled carelessly off its back-side spurted an occasional squirt of water. Each of the knobby tires that supported the truck was shoulder-high and made of hardened rubber that surrounded a thick hub of steel.

As he drew closer the figure became clearer, and Jimmy realized that he was inspecting a teenager on her way home from school. He let out a wry, gap-toothed smile and pulled his grimy baseball cap down over his chubby melon, as if he was trying to hide his identity. He relaxed back in his seat, but he kept a wandering eye on Little Jennifer Gables. Then Jimmy stomped the accelerator down with his foot and nudged the speedometer of his laden beast past forty-five.

The wind blew Little Jennifer's flaxen hair off her slender shoulders, and her long, purposeful strides revealed that her destination was close by. The afternoon traffic cluttered the airwaves around her, and the rusty leaves that littered the sidewalk scrambled in frantic circles, as if they were looking for a place to hide.

Jimmy noticed a vibration in the steering wheel, and he looked down at his trembling hands, as if they held some sort of explanation. He felt the truck lurch and stutter, but did not see one of his rig's massive rear tires separate from its axle. Nor did he see it peel off to the side and travel on its course; a course determined by force and by chance…

…and the tire bounced further on up the road.

We struggle sometimes with how to live our lives, so we do our best to follow a set of rules. Be good. Be kind. Be loyal. Be God-fearing. "God has a plan for us," we are told by those who preach, teach, fear, and hope. Believe and your faith will be rewarded.

But sometimes these words ring hollow when the world's dirty deeds unfold before us. This was the case when Little Jennifer Gables was killed by the runaway wheel from a cement truck, and the people of town were left to try to make sense of the senseless. Sometimes it seems there is God, and sometimes not.

Little Jennifer Gables had brought death to their hometown. Not a death attached to a foreign cause or celebrated event (like the names etched into the stone monument on the common). It was an up close and accidental death, and it took away the promise of tomorrow. The people were forced to ask themselves the unanswerable: Why?

So they gathered with candles and flowers at the sight of the accident, and with sadness at Emerson's Funeral Home (the line stretched across First Street and under the common's massive oak trees). They brought food and comfort to the home of the grieving Gables, joined together in sorrow for the service at the

Congregational Church, and dutifully assembled when her body was lowered into the ground at the town cemetery.

Then the grays of the late November sky faded into blackness. The people of town moved on. Time removed Little Jennifer from their midst.

Those who knew her best tried to keep her memory alive, and they all certainly missed her and all that she never got to be. But what the townspeople never forgot about that day was that Little Jennifer's lemonade stand and trips to the savings bank stopped, the way her open school books fluttered in the wind on the sidewalk next to a solitary shoe, and that another seat opened up forever at the Gables' dinner table.

Mrs. Gables had once traveled the roads of her hometown armed with her faith and the promise of better days. She rose up early in the morning, worked hard, and tried to live her family's life the right way. But among the promise of the rural roads that surrounded her, Mrs. Gables found darkness. She lost a child.

For a time she stumbled among the shadows. Then she pushed herself back out onto the very same streets that robbed her of that promise. Somehow, Mrs. Gables found a reason to believe that she would find light among the darkness and see her Little Jennifer again…someday, further on up the road.

BARN BURNING, '73

Slim's real name was Jeffrey, but everyone in town called him Slim Shady - "Slim" because his frame was wiry, like a fuse. But also, because at age nine he began stealing his mother's Virginia Slim cigarettes and stashing them in key locations about town, to light them up later.

"Shady" came soon after, because despite his slim stature, he cast a long and dark shadow wherever he went. If you saw Slim skulking about town, you usually saw him with his hands in his pockets, head looking down at the tops of his shoes, and a cigarette dangling from his lower lip.

Slim thought he was a tough little bastard.

Slim Shady was now twenty-two, and he stood in the quaint but busy center of town on a sidewalk that ran along the corner of Main and Cross Street, diagonal from the town's Congregational Church. He leaned back, with his arms folded across his chest and with one foot on the ground the other with its sole up against the fieldstone wall that defined the boundary of Mrs. Dodd's property line.

Smoke drifted out of his lungs like the afternoon sun that radiated off the black pavement of the intersecting streets before him. The wall Slim leaned against wrapped itself around the inside edge of the sidewalk and ran down both streets. The summer hayfield that sat above it was tall and still.

This location was known as The Corner – the place where The Trouble Kids hung out, smoked, and swore. Small towns are small places, and when the kids in town had nothing to do they did nothing at The Corner. Slim Shady started hanging out there shortly after smoking his first Virginia Slim, and it never occurred to him to stop going there. The Corner was his sanctuary.

Slim's blonde hair draped over his ears. His wedge-like nose was framed by high-set cheek bones that were covered with acne - a condition that plagued him since puberty. On his boney left tricep, just below the sleeve of his unbuttoned shirt was a tattoo of a clenched up fist. The fist's knuckles were jutting out and its fingers were curled and folded tightly down - save for the middle one. Slim's black ink tattoo was giving the finger to you, me, his mother, and the rest of the world. But what lay unseen and unknown to all of us was the hole in Slim Shady's heart.

What was well known, was Slim. He was one of those Trouble Kids and at age eight he was caught breaking bottles against the wall behind the church. At nine he squirted shaving cream in Billy Curley's eyes while trick-or-treating. At ten, he was caught stealing a fist-full of penny candy from Harland's Hardware, and by fifteen he had a penchant for sipping from a smuggled Pabst Blue Ribbon beer can (hidden inside of a paper bag) while riding about town on his green 10-speed Schwinn bicycle. But Slim's biggest transgression came when, at the age of sixteen, he struck a match to some hay that lay at the base of his family's barn.

At the time of the fire, Slim's parents owned a

modest sized horse farm, two miles out of the town's center. His dad was a simple man - one who preferred to work in solitude as his own stable manager than to interact with the people who boarded their horses at his barn. Slim's parents owned three equines of their own and rented out the remaining stalls.

His father enjoyed the barn. Each day he got up in the morning and went to work, coming back to the house for meals and returning to finish the day's work until darkness dictated his day's end. Slim's father lived for himself, and that made it hard on everyone in the family.

Life inside the barn was much easier than it was outside. Humans being human can make life messy sometimes and Slim's father did not like messes. Instead of dealing with the full catastrophe of his life, his father put his head down and went about things the way he wanted.

Slim's mother had little use for the barn, and she developed resentment for what it meant to her husband. Over the years she came to sarcastically call it, "The Church" because, in her own words, "He worshipped the damn thing like it was home to God himself!" Slim's mother worked at the public library during the day and did their books at night – and that fueled the resentment even more. Boarding horses was a lot of work with little gain - none in the last three quarters according to her ledger.

This is not how she saw her life playing out. Slim's mother abandoned her own dreams a long time ago and was left with the reality of dreams unfulfilled. Now - more than ever - she needed someone or something to believe in, and it had begun to occur to her that she would wind up with nothing and nobody. Disappointment can breed resentment, and Slim's mother had turned bitter, and she took it out on the ones she loved.

On the morning of the fire, Slim had stashed three of his mother's Virginia Slims in an old Wonder Bread bag around the back side of the barn. It was where the horses' manure and the mud formed a soupy mixture and turned it into a place that nobody went. Nobody except Slim Shady. The cigarettes were there, on standby, should he need an elixir.

That evening, Slim quietly and purposefully left the house. His parents were going at it again. They argued often, but almost always on Thursday nights when his father was in the house and when his mother opened their books and paid their bills.

Darkness had descended and dinner had long been over when things escalated. Slim had heard enough and went outside to get some relief. "Christ" he murmured to himself as he slipped out the front door and into the moonlight. Neither parent heard the sound of the door's latch as it fell back into place.

Slim craved the taste of the tobacco but never more than when he was coming out of his house. As he approached the old bread bag that lay tucked between the stack of hay bales at the base of the barn, he could not wait to feel the thin tube of paper roll between his fingers or taste the dried tobacco flakes....He needed it. He craved it

The sound a match makes when it is struck is a powerful one, and for a smoker it can mirror the rush one feels when the nicotine unloads itself into the body. Both the sound of the matchstick igniting and the sensation of the chemical are addicting in their own ways, and when Slim inserted the cigarette between his lips and struck the match, his body was in anticipation sensory overload.

Slim Shady put the lit match to the end of his cigarette, pursed his lips together as if he were kissing a loved-one (he was), and sucked in. The release and relief that came with the drag was soothing - satisfaction was literally on the tip of his tongue and on its way to his body and his brain. As Slim inhaled his first breath of smoke, he heard his mother's shrill tones ring out from the house and shatter the night's silence, like a bolt of lightning.

"You and your damn church can go to hell because that's where I've been living for the last eighteen years!" He could not make out his father's muffled response.

They ruined it again - his moment of happiness. With the match still lit in one hand and the glow of the Virginia Slim in the other, the thought came to him peacefully and quietly, as if the idea were handed down by a greater power. Slim exhaled, and the smoke streamed out of his mouth like steam from a singing kettle. He took his lit matchstick with the flame nearing his fingertips, and quite deliberately let it drop.

"Screw you," he said - to nobody and to everybody. Then he turned his back on the barn and began to walk away.

Slim's satisfaction wore off quickly when he heard the flickering flame crackle in the still of the warm summer night, and it gave way to panic when he turned around to see the dried out hay on the side of the barn in flames. Slim's new reality began to set in, and panic turned to hysteria as he tried to beat the flames into submission with his shirt, without success.

Fire took over the dried-out pine siding on the barn, as well as the shirt he was trying to snuff it out with. Things were burning out of control, and on impulse he dropped everything, including the lit cigarette from his mouth, and ran – through the mud and manure, past the electric fence that lined the fields where his father turned out the horses, and away from the mess he made.

Slim's lungs burned and screamed at him to quit

running, but he kept on going, using the silvery glow of the moon as his guiding light until he finally reached his family's property line. Slim dove bare-chested and head-first over a rock wall and hid under cover of thorny raspberry bushes and sprigs of poison ivy. He turned on his bloodied elbows and looked back at the barn in disbelief. The night sky was glowing, and Slim couldn't help but admire the silhouette of the barn and the contrast of the red and orange flames in the blackness of the dark. Spires of fire were licking up the barn's back wall and fanning outwards as it looked for more fuel. White smoke unrolled itself in billows and surges, and then disappeared as it became one with the night.

Every child has committed an act that was impulsive or selfish. Many of us, in a panic, have run away and hoped that our actions would go unnoticed, or that the results of our actions would disappear. Many of us - as we fled - swore to God that we would never do it again.

For Slim Shady that moment was now. Slim was scared – terrified of what he had done and what would happen to him when it was discovered. He wanted to tell his parents about their barn burning, but he could not bring himself to do it...because he could not explain why he did it - to them or to anyone, not even himself. So Slim froze. He hid and he watched his family's barn burning. The sixteen year old boy who thought himself so bad – the tough little bastard that he thought he was – was really afraid.

It was not his father's blood curdling scream upon discovering the inferno. Nor was it his feeble attempts to douse the flames with the garden hose or his mother's frantic calls of, "Spray the house! Don't let it spread to the house! Forget the barn!" that made it happen.

As Slim lay crouched on his elbows and knees in the darkness, with his butt down below the sightline of the rock wall, it was the sound of the horses that got to him. Their whinnying was frantic, their metal shoes clattered on the barn's wooden floor, and the gates to their stalls banged as they desperately crashed and kicked what they knew was their only exit from the choking smoke and searing heat. That's when his senses became too much for him bear. Slim started to cry.

The realization that he could not take back what he had done – compounded by the sudden realization as to why he had done it – was too much. Slim spent much of his life getting and giving little love, and he never truly realized it until that moment. When it struck him, it did so cruelly. Slim realized that he cared more for the horses inside the barn than the people who ran around it, and the anguish that spewed forth from this realization left his lips quivering.

Slim rose up on his knees and buried his head down into his chest, and gripped his shaggy long hair with his fists and began to sob. What poured out of his scrawny little frame began as a whine, but soon escalated to sobs of long, drawn out regret and moans of self-loathing.

The sound of sorrow poured out from Slim Shady, and it carried over the grass fields and into the darkness, where it was drowned out by the crackling of the pine boards and angry roar of the fire. Nobody, not his parents, the horses in the barn, or the volunteer fire department that just arrived heard Slim as he let loose an anguished cry of, "Why'd you make me like I am?"

If someone had heard him they would not have known who Slim was talking to – his parents, maybe God? Perhaps both.

You can rebuild a barn, and that's what Slim's mother and father did. Three horses died in the fire and all were owned by Slim's family. The six that were rescued or escaped were boarders – intentionally placed in the front stalls of the barn so that the owners would stay away from Slim's father's workshop in the back.

The fire was ruled an accident, but Slim's disappearance and the barn burning were easy dots to connect. Slim slipped away for a few days, staying in the woods and abandoned barns that lay along the rural road connecting his home to the town's center and The Corner – the very spot where he now stood.

Slim went down another notch in everybody's eyes, and while the damage done to his own property was repairable, the damage that Slim had done to himself was not. The barn burning was added to the list of wrongs committed by Slim Shady. Blame is an easy thing to assign. Indicting another person can also set one's self free: Slim lit a match and he burned a barn down. Case closed.

All around town, families talked about the barn burning over supper, mothers picking up prescriptions at the drugstore recounted the tale to each other at the counter (as if they were there themselves), and the news spread like a flame does to the thin paper covering of a cigarette. As each citizen had their Judgment Day, Slim took the blame again and again.

Nobody (including his parents) forgave Slim. For Slim Shady, no forgiveness meant no redemption, and Slim was forced to live with and carry his guilt.

In the six years since he burned his parent's barn down to the ground, Slim Shady went nowhere. But Slim no longer hated everyone else, like the tattoo on his arm suggested. What Slim hated was who he was and what he had turned out to be. As he leaned back, uncomfortably, against Mrs. Dodd's fieldstone wall, the cars on Main Street passed him by and their passengers failed to notice Slim, or chose not to. Slim may have been standing at a crossroads, but his path was determined a long time ago.

The townspeople knew all about Slim Shady and the trouble his shadow brought with him, and they all certainly knew about his family's barn burning. But nobody knew about the hole in Slim Shady's heart.

LUCKY IN THIS TOWN, '74

On Sunday morning Tom White swung his legs over the side of the bed and onto the hardwood floor. He leaned forward with his elbows on his knees and rubbed his eye sockets with his palms, trying to rid himself of the morning fog.

His mood reflected the weather system that slid in from the coast as he and Mary were going to bed, and he could hear the rainwater as it ran down the roof and splashed into the gutters. The wind driven drops pelted at the windows, and the morning air inside and outside of their colonial style New England home was raw.

Tom tried to rise quietly, and when he glanced back to measure his success he paused to look at Mary. Her head was turned off to the side and lay softly submerged within her pillow. The white cotton quilt was up to her neck and her long and delicate arms rested on top, framing the sides of her tiny profile. At one time her hair was jet black, but it now shaded gradual grays. He could not help but notice that even in her sleep Mary was elegant.

The shifting of his weight on the floor emitted a creak from the joists underneath his feet and from the joints within his knees. He could see Mary's eyelids flutter open. Tom turned away and shuffled off down the hall to the bathroom to the shower. Church services began at ten o'clock. Another day was underway.

The steam from the shower quickly replaced the coldness of the bathroom. He enjoyed the shelter and the warmth that it provided, and as he scrubbed his face clean the soap began to sting his eyes. Tom blindly reached for one of the many facecloths piled on the side of the shower, and in his haste he knocked over several of Mary's shampoos. This in turn sent her razor and other bathroom gadgetry off the shelf and onto the tub floor. Swearing, he knelt down and clumsily tried to collect and place them back where they belonged - all while seeking relief from the still stinging soap. By the time he found a suitable facecloth, the door burst open and the moist warm air that was once contained escaped.

The disruption was quickly followed by the clink of the toilet seat and the sound of a pee stream.

"Ahhh. Hi Daddy!" shouted Samuel, Tom and Mary's six year old, and the youngest of their three boys.

Irritated at the intrusion of his solitude, but resigned to its inevitability, Tom responded, "Hi Samuel. Make sure you shut the door tight after you leave, ok?"

"Okay Daddy! "

Before Tom could say, "And please don't flush." Samuel flushed.

The hot water surge scalded Tom's chest and he jumped back in an arch so that only his toes suffered. He was always on his boys for not flushing so he reasoned that now was not the time to be mad at Samuel for remembering.

"Don't forget today is Pancake Day!" Samuel called

out, neglecting to wash his hands and leaving the door wide open behind him. The comfort of the warm steam continued to elude Tom as it cascaded and rolled out into the hallway.

The Whites made their way to the breakfast table at their own pace. Mary waited until Tom was clear of the upstairs before she slipped out of her nightgown and into her Sunday dress. Samuel, having gone back to bed and become lost in his GI Joes, had to be summoned. Middle child Matthew had been curled up in the living room under a blanket reading a library copy of *Encyclopedia Brown Takes the Case.* Sixteen year old Luke was up and ready for church before anyone else - waiting at the table dressed in his Sunday best, complete with a healthy dose of Tom's Aqua Velva aftershave.

Tradition called for a family breakfast on Sunday mornings and the boys took turns choosing the menu. Samuel always chose pancakes and Tom always cooked so that Mary could have the morning off. The smell of Tom's pancakes on the griddle and the clinking of silverware filled the air. To Samuel the silence was unbearable - because it just was - so he decided to break it.

"Luke, why were you sucking on Jenny's face in the cemetery?"

Stunned, Luke just stared at Samuel, wishing he could shove the words right back in his mouth. But it was too late, and the awkward silence returned, tenfold.

Tom jumped in to save all, including himself, and before he could hear anymore said, "Samuel, we are in the middle of Sunday breakfast. That's not an appropriate discussion topic."

Tom knew Luke had been hanging around Jenny Savage, but to hear Samuel's account of just how close the relationship actually was came as a bit of a surprise. Tom remembered being that age, and he both envied and pitied Luke. His son, the young man, was unaware that the age of innocence would be replaced by his own age of reality.

Samuel couldn't understand why his dad did not want to know why Luke was sucking Jenny's face in the cemetery so he served a follow-up question. "But

Dad, why would anyone do that? Luke's lips were…"

"Samuel. *Enough!*" scolded Tom. Samuel knew another follow up might result in an early dismissal from Pancake Day so he frowned, stabbed a stack with his fork, and slumped back in his chair to make the most of what was left on his plate.

"No more cemetery discussion." stated Tom, trying to sound stern and in control.

Mary silently picked up her dish and walked over to the trash and scraped off the remnants of her half-eaten pancake. As she plopped the syrupy plate into the sink-full of soapy water she contemplated how the conversation with Luke would go when she inquired about what else went on in the cemetery. She also made a mental note to ask Samuel what made him think it was ok to ride his bike where it meant he had to cross Main Street without an adult - a forbidden act.

Matthew, aware that the focus was on his brothers, took another forkful of pancake and slid Encyclopedia Brown up from under the table and onto his lap, and continued reading.

"Finish up. It's nearly nine-thirty and we don't want

to be late." Mary instructed. Mary was the poise and grace that the boys in the family did not always have, so while they pushed themselves away from the table and scrambled to finish getting ready for church she calmly took a collection envelope out from the junk drawer and filled it with a check. Soon the Whites gathered together again in the kitchen, and as they packed into the wood paneled Ford Country Squire station wagon they found going to church a welcome distraction - each for different reasons.

The White's wagon pulled out of the driveway and Tom drove towards the center of town and the Congregational Church. The coldness of the car's seats made them stiff and unforgiving, and the air smelled of Luke's Aqua Velva. The Ford's windshield wipers worked overtime and whined and clicked accordingly, and as Tom headed past the common, the Town Hall, and the cemetery (the scene of Luke's crime of passion), he thought about how he wound up here.

Tom grew up in this town, like his father before him, and as a boy he never gave much thought to growing old anywhere else. But it was assumed by most (not by Tom) that he would someday take over the family's clamming business and that is exactly what he did - and it happened sooner than anyone had anticipated.

Tom was only twenty at the time (just a bit older than Luke was now) and he remembered the warm July evening when Dr. Bartlett sat on their living room sofa and gently told them that Dad had pancreatic cancer and would only have a few months left for living. He also remembered how strange it was that words so shattering - so seemingly apocalyptic - could be stated so matter-of-factly. They were not accompanied by dramatic background music or preserved in a photograph like so many other signature moments in a life. Instead, Dr. Bartlett's words hung in the air and then vanished - no different than small-talk or a mundane observation, and when the words he uttered were gone, they left only their reality behind.

Tom remembered how when Dr. Bartlett left them that night, the screen door on the front porch snapped shut, and it shattered the stillness of the night air and seemed to trigger his mother and sisters to crying. But he himself failed to understand the true consequences of the good Doctor's words, and Tom was ashamed to admit that all he felt at that time was fear and a perverse curiosity.

It was only after his dad died that sadness and regret poured in. To young Tom, death seemed like a magic trick – God's cruel magic trick. He saw his father disappear before his very eyes, and he was left to wonder how it all could be.

Tom let college slide off the books, and he dutifully assumed control of White's Shellfish Company. While his dad's death left a void in the business and in his family's collective heart, Tom tried to fill the obligation he felt to both. Sometimes he did it well and sometimes he struggled. He and Mary had gone steady since high school and they eventually set up shop and family in the very same house that Tom himself was raised in. His mom moved into the Cape across the street, next to the Company's small processing and packaging plant, and life went on. Tom pushed both the family and the business ahead. Looking back after all these years, he was never sure if it was the path he chose, or if the path was chosen for him.

This particular fall brought a new challenge to White's Shellfish and to all the local shellfish companies. In September the shellfish beds in the Atlantic were shut down due to a natural but deadly phenomenon, given an obvious name by the media, Red Tide. Sample any sea water and you will find microscopic creatures and algae, and if the conditions are right they can create enormous blooms of a magnificent scope. This summer a new creature settled into the waters off New England and turned the waters a dead red.

Those who understood the sea knew that Alexandrium Tamarense could be found in the waters off the coast of Maine and Canada, but this year it crept south. As clams, mussels, oysters, and scallops siphoned and filtered this particular phytoplankton laden seawater through their organs each day they collected the poison inside, and while the shellfish themselves remained unaffected, the human beings who ingested the carrier (cooked or raw) also ingested the poison. The invisible Alexandrium Tamarense could render the seafood lover paralyzed or dead, and clam beds were shut down, boats remained docked, delivery trucks sat empty at their loading bays, and Red Tide led to red ink in the ledgers of shellfish companies all over New England.

Tom was in the middle of a struggle to save his company, and as he drove his family to church that morning he felt the full weight of his responsibilities.

Through the smeared wipers and the hard rain Tom could see the pointed white church steeple looming ahead. He snuck a glance at his own reflection in the rear view mirror and silently acknowledged that his youth had given way. The Country Squire made its way under the town's only traffic light and slowed as it passed the front of the white pillared church. The family wagon made the turn into the church parking lot.

The congregation was assembling.

The Whites parked in their usual space and hurried towards the shelter of the church as the wind pushed at their backs. They filed up the long slate steps, between the tall white columns, and under the steeple that housed the giant clock and ringing bell.

Upon entering the narthex they shook the rain from their coats and then hands with the morning greeters who handed out the Sunday bulletins - the scent of the mimeograph machine's ink was still strong.

To their left, in a dated brown suit, Deacon Faulkner was stoically pulling the thick, braided rope that threaded its way down from the bell tower, through the ceiling, and into his white gloved hands. The tall, silver haired elder statesmen of the church pulled the rope down so that its full length coiled onto the floor, and as he released the rope it uncoiled and went back up through his guiding hands and into the ceiling. With each pull, the bell rocked and rang.

Samuel wriggled free of Mary's hand and cut over to Deacon Faulkner and asked directly, "Can I ring the bell?" Deacon Faulkner was not one to tolerate playing in God's house, but he saw the gaze of others upon him and felt obligated to give the boy a turn, so he let go of the rope and issued instructions in a slow, gravelly voice.

"Reach up as high as you can and grip the rope tightly. Pull it down as low as you can and then let it slide back up through your hands. Don't grip it too tight or the friction will burn."

After a few assisted pulls, Deacon Faulkner stepped back. Samuel pulled the rope himself.

"Look Dad, I'm doing it!" Curling his tongue out between his lips he prepared to give the rope another yank. Samuel's bell ringing was the last call for the congregation. The doors would be closing soon, and a late entrance would result in turned heads and passed judgment.

Tom was afraid Samuel would be too much for the Deacon so he made his way over to the odd couple should anything go wrong.

"Nice Sam. You are doing a great job." he said, reminding each one that he was nearby.

"Thanks! I'm pulling so hard I'm gonna crack it!" Samuel replied.

Glancing over at a frowning Deacon Faulkner, Tom decided it was time to step in, so he took another step closer with his hand outstretched and said, "Okay, that's plenty of ringing. Let's get to our seats."

Samuel was bending over in a follow-through from his most recent attempt to crack the bell, and upon hearing his fun was over he stood up quickly and looked at his dad. Scowling, he gripped and pulled the rope tight in defiance and whined, "Aw, can't I do one more?"

As the rope ascended it went taught, and Samuel and was pulled up and off the floor in a flash. Tom was left staring at Samuel's dangling shoe-tops. He reached up and plucked Samuel from the sky before he came crashing down.

"Thanks Deacon." mumbled a sheepish, retreating Tom. Deacon Faulkner frowned and shook his head in quiet disapproval, and collected the rope and tethered it to the wall. Samuel told Tom he wanted "to go for another ride on the rope," as the Whites took their usual place in their usual pew.

The walls and woodwork inside this old Protestant church were painted a bright white and all the trim stained a deep brown. A red carpet ran up both sides of the sanctuary and split the pews down the center aisle. At the front of the sanctuary were three steps that led to a landing that served as access to the pulpit and choir pews. In the back of the landing, under the organ pipes, was a long communion table surrounded by two tall brass candelabras.

The table was used once every month and had "In Remembrance of Me," written calligraphy style in gold letters across its facing.

Reverend Rogers led the congregation in sermon and prayer, and organist Marge Thompson led them in music and song. The service was a standard affair for the Whites. Tom doubted the existence of God while Mary embraced it. Luke worshiped at the altar of Jenny, Samuel struggled to suppress his desire to walk and talk throughout, and Matthew continued his escape with Encyclopedia Brown, using his bulletin as a book-cover.

The premise of Reverend Rogers' sermon was posed to the congregation in the form of a question, "How do we know there is a God?" The Reverend cited the Book of Exodus and the acts it contained of God revealing or manifesting himself, which made seeing and believing (and fearing) an easy proposition. The burning bush and the turning of a staff into a serpent were tangible proof of God's voice and will. "Where are the signs today?" he asked them.

"Look around you a little bit closer," Reverend Rogers suggested. "The signs are there, we just need to keep an open mind and eye as they present themselves." Despite the good Reverend's best efforts, a skeptical Tom found it easier to see proof God did not exist, rather than any sign that he did. Tom went through the motions singing, "Faith of Our Fathers," with the rest of the congregation, and he wondered if the modern day plague of Red Tide was his own punishment for not completely believing – for doubting. The ocean, once his escape, had become his haunting.

The day his mother asked him to scatter his dad's ashes into the Atlantic was almost one year after Doctor Bartlett came to their home, and several months after his father had died. She told him his father wanted his remains to be buried in the family plot at the town cemetery and a portion to be cast into the sea. His mother instructed him to gather the boys from the shop and finish the job.

On a sunny afternoon in the middle of July, Tom and the grown men of White's Shellfish Company launched a company boat from Smitty's Marina at the town landing, and piloted their vessel a few miles offshore. Tom cut the engine and let the boat drift among the rolling waves, and in the haze of the heavy summer sun he said a few clumsy words and opened the urn. Tom leaned over the side and scattered his father into the deep green sea.

When he did so, he felt more like a Betrayer than a Trustee.

One of the men emptied the contents of a half-full bottle of Scotch into six styrofoam cups which were distributed to a man. Larry was originally hired by Tom's father to clean the shucking tables and wash down the plant after each day's work, and he was limited in his abilities and still lived with his elderly parents. He carried with him the faint scent of garlic, and when he talked his voice sounded as if he was trying to suppress a laugh.

In the awkward silence that followed the scattering of the ashes it was Larry who raised his cup to the summer sky and said with a chortled voice, "To Sam. Whatever will be, will be." Tom remembered how tears streamed silently down Larry's cheeks as he tipped his head back and swallowed his harsh offering.

When the Sunday service was over, the congregation filed out in a crowded shuffle, shaking hands with Reverend Rogers upon their exit. As he stepped out from the shelter of the church, Tom noticed how the people spilled out into driveway like sheep filtering out of a pen in a mad scramble, until the faithful flock rounded the side of the building and broke ranks as they headed to their cars.

Turning into the wind, Mary tightened the belt of her dress-coat, pushed her long wet hair off to the side, and raised her umbrella to block out the driving rain. She met the storm head-on and pulled a fidgety Samuel closer by putting a hand on his shoulder.

"Come on. Let's get out of this mess."

An umbrella-less Tom was dragging behind and the rain had already soaked his head and the shoulders of his overcoat. While Mary's pace had quickened, Tom's had slowed. He reached into his trouser pocket and pulled out his car keys and stood still.

"Mary." He said loudly, in order to be heard above the din of the rain as it pounded the pavement and umbrellas.

Mary stopped and turned in one smooth, deliberate motion, and while she said nothing the expression on her face asked, "What?"

Holding his keys between his forefinger and thumb he held them out towards her at arm's length, taking a couple of steps closer to Mary.

Assuming he wanted her to drive or that he had left something behind in the sanctuary, Mary reached for the keys.

"I'll meet you at home. I want to walk," said Tom.

"What are you talking about? It's pouring out," said Mary in disbelief.

"I'll be fine. It's not that far." Tom responded, taking the path of least resistance.

Cold and wet, and tired of weathering the storm, Mary's jaw dropped open. She took the keys with a quick fist and coldly said, "Take my umbrella then."

"I'll be fine," replied Tom.

"Come on, we are getting soaked," Mary said to the boys.

Matthew closed his soggy book and took notice of the changing fronts. Samuel remained quiet for once, and Luke wondered if this would impact his earlier request to go over to Jenny's to do homework.

Tom turned his back on his family and began walking home, crossing back in front of the Church, over Cross Street, and on to the sidewalk of Main. His mopped hair was plastered to his head and tears of rain streamed down his face. Tom picked his head up and looked around.

The town center and its shops and markets were virtually unchanged over the years. He recalled hopping into his dad's pick-up truck as a boy and coming here for their Saturday morning errands. They'd walk together proudly and say, "Good morning" to the folks they met along the way. Now, Tom walked passed these places alone and in the rain. He remembered the day his father put his hands on his shoulders and said, "Son, we're lucky in this town."

As Tom made his way in front of the post office he heard the angry hum of the Country Squire coming from behind. When the family car splashed by he looked up. A deserted Main Street was one large puddle and the bubbly tracks laid out by the car quickly flooded over.

The two red taillights of the Ford glowed in the misty morning rain, and inside the foggy rear window of the Country Squire Tom could see the blurred figure of young Samuel looking back at him.

Tom sighed, and to a question never posed he answered aloud, "This is what will be."

THE GREAT DIVIDE, '75

As a nine year old boy, Billy Jackson was a lot of things. He was fast on his feet and quick with his thoughts. He was a scoundrel to his little sister and still a baby to his mother. He showed no fear to those who meant him harm, yet he was afraid to go to bed without his nightlight.

Billy Jackson was a lot like you and me.

He moved into town in late summer, and shortly thereafter attended the first day of school on a Wednesday morning in early September. When Billy's worn down high top sneakers crossed through the doorway of Whispering Pines Elementary School, he walked right through a threshold that, up until that moment, had remained unnoticed and uncrossed.

Billy was black, and he was the first real "person of

color" to enter Whispering Pines. His skin and closely cropped curly hair were black like the night, and the whites of his eyes were punctuated with deep black pigments in the center. His eyes burned bright like a pair of white-hot stars ablaze and alone in a darkened galaxy. Billy was Boston Black, and the coastal New England town in which he now lived was Yankee White.

Despite being a lot like you and me on the inside, Billy was different from every other child who set foot in the school before him. These are the facts of the matter.

Autumn is a time of great change in New England. Those who live there tend to accept (if not embrace) the falling temperatures and shorter days with a stoic, quiet optimism. They know that the impending pall of winter that soon follows is inevitable, to endure it is a birthright, and to accept its hardship without complaint shows a defiant strength and a willingness to wait for the rebirth and rewards of spring.

The autumn before Billy arrived at Whispering Pines, the winds of change blew stronger and more deliberate, and a storm spun over the region and changed things as they were - and turned order into chaos.

In June of 1974, in the great state of Massachusetts (a state which took pride in sharing the common wealth), US District Judge Arthur Garrity ruled that the city of Boston had systematically segregated its neighborhoods – and therefore its schools - by race. His ruling demanded that in order to comply with the laws governing this nation, the city must desegregate.

It was time to change.

This time, change in Boston did not come easy. Judge Garrity's ruling meant it was time to rip off the Band-Aid. White students and black students were uprooted from their neighborhood schools and bused to other neighborhood schools, far from their familiar streets, teachers, and faces.

For one whole year the city that identified itself as the "Birthplace of Liberty" burned with rage and smoldered with widespread resentment and pockets of violence. Indelible images and detailed accounts of the discourse and confrontation between poor blacks in

Mattapan and poor whites in Dorchester were recorded for the world to see.

Bottles and rocks were thrown by angry white mobs in South Boston at arriving black students from Roxbury. Local politicians, the press, and law enforcement stirred the pot, and the stew of human emotions went from a simmer to a rolling boil. Everybody had an opinion. Everybody knew who was to blame.

Through it all, Billy's new town observed and contemplated these problems from afar and thought them a great mess. Thankfully, the issue of race was "down the road a piece" - far enough so that if it made them uncomfortable, they only had to look away.

When Billy, his sister, and mother moved into town to escape the hell of busing in Boston, they were hardened and wise. When they arrived in town early that summer, there were no violent outbursts or protests, and life in the small town was relaxed and simple before - and it remained that way after.

But people, as we tend to do, took notice of those who are different, and the unrest that continued to drag on in Boston one year later crept from the back of their minds and to the front of their thoughts. The Jacksons' arrival got folks to wondering and thinking, and many (including Billy's classmates) had to stare race in the face for the very first time.

This is the climate in which Billy was now enrolled.

Billy's first few mornings at Whispering Pines were uneventful. But on the first Friday morning recess, he walked as fast as he could to the back door of his classroom, being careful not to run. Mrs. Shyne made any rule-breaker return to his seat and, "Try it again."

When he made it out the door, Billy scrambled up the fifteen cement steps that led to a plateau that served as the playground. He headed right for the swings. There were thirty-two third graders at Whispering Pines, but only enough swings for eight at a time. On that day, Billy was fast enough to claim one of them for himself.

Kathleen Lyons was a recess aide and she wore a metal whistle around her neck, and she loved the power she imagined it gave her. She let out a shrill short burst of "tweet!" every two minutes, as a signal to the swingers that it was time to get off and to let another eight children have their turn.

Two minutes is not a long time, especially for a third grader on a swing. From the minute Billy and his seven lucky classmates backed up onto the stiff concave rubber seats and plopped themselves down they began pumping, leaning back as the swing rushed forward, and pulling with all their might on the chains to increase their speed. By the time maximum height was obtained their stomachs fluttered, and each swinger watched Mrs. Lyons intently as she glanced at her watch and massaged the whistle between her fingers. She ran the show, and they knew they had better move quickly when she blew.

On her signal, all eight first-graders took one last pump, and as they alternately soared forward, they jumped. Billy landed cleanly and immediately cut to his left, off to wait his turn at the monkey bars. As he did, Lawrence Hicks was nervously preparing to make his own leap, but he was forced into an awkward abort lest he collide with Billy. Clutching the metal chains tightly in his fists Lawrence slipped off the seat and dragged his shoes through the underlying, loose dirt letting fly a cloud of dust.

It was a brief but obvious and embarrassing moment for Lawrence, witnessed by Mrs. Lyons, all the children still on their swings, and by those waiting their turn. Billy let out a quick, "Sorry" and looked at the dangling, hanging Lawrence. He paused for a moment, sensing his classmate was about to say something.

For as long as he could remember, in times of trouble or sadness, Billy's mom would often give him a hug, pat him on the back, and tell him, "There is a time to cry and a time to forget it."

Billy had finished crying over being called names a long time ago. He knew that bottles and rocks cause the real pain. So, when he heard what Lawrence Hicks called him, Billy smirked and raced off to the monkey bars, to where more important matters awaited. Billy was unaware that Lawrence's word spun a series of subtle disturbances for those he left behind.

Mrs. Lyons grew up in South Boston and her brother Sean and his two teenage sons still lived there.

Sean worked for wages as a welder at the Quincy Shipyard to support his boys and melancholy wife. Mrs. Lyons had left Southie, hoping to find a better life, but Sean chose to stay and endure. He still said his Hail Mary's at the Gate of Heaven Parish, and his boys attended a desegregated (but highly divided) South Boston High School.

Southie was a poor but proud borough of Boston - a working class neighborhood. The people who lived there were not given much, and anything they got was earned at the expense of their backs - but not their spirit. They looked out for each other because nobody else would, and the solidarity among its people was absolute. The city wore a chip on its collective shoulder, as they felt they had everything to lose, and if anyone - or anything - came between them, it got their Irish up.

As Mrs. Lyons watched black students from Dorchester get bused into South Boston High School, and as she witnessed all of the violence that ensued, she blamed desegregation on the Government and on the blacks for making her family's problems - Southie's problems - worse.

She had no issue with black students having better schools but, "Two wrongs don't make a right" she'd say when the topic came up. However, when she heard the word Lawrence Hicks called Billy Jackson it was impossible for her to overlook. She loved Southie, but her heart was no longer in it.

She was tired of the fighting - and decided it was time to put a stop to it. Mrs. Lyons blew the whistle on Lawrence Hicks and brought him to the principal's office by his ear.

Kelly and Joanna were impatiently waiting their turn for a swing when Lawrence said his piece to Billy Jackson. Joanna had strong convictions for a third grader, and a strong sense of self. She was repulsed by the word she heard come from Lawrence's mouth, but she also knew that when Mrs. Lyons had you by the ear you would not get away with your misdeed - Lawrence would get what he deserved. Joanna hopped on her swing and began pumping.

Kelly, on the other hand, was taken in by other people's suffering, perhaps a bit too easily. Her parents referred to themselves as, "hippies" and talked with shame about the wrongs committed by whites against blacks throughout this country's history. As a result, Kelly felt responsible for the pain she thought Billy felt - she felt guilty for being who she was. She followed Billy over to the monkey bars and tried to make him laugh, hoping that it would make him (and her) feel better. She was unaware that it was not necessary.

Lawrence Hicks got into trouble. When Principal Chase called Lawrence's mother at home to tell her of the playground incident, Mrs. Hicks sighed impatiently and asked if he didn't have more important things to do than call her about two boys who had an argument on the playground. What was the big deal?

When the Principal told her that Lawrence should not attend school on Monday it became a big deal, and when Mr. Hicks got home from work he reached for his belt and gave Lawrence something to think about. He would've rather used it on the kid who caused the trouble in the first place, and maybe even on the principal, but Lawrence would have to do. As Mr. Hicks' belt left its mark on his legacy, Lawrence hated

Billy Jackson even more, and secretly loved the attention his father was giving him.

This is an old story - not the story of *Billy Jackson vs. Lawrence Hicks* or of *Black vs. White*. It is the story of the human condition. Storms are spun and they pound the generations as they come and go. The currents between our differences ebb and flow but never seem to disappear. Each generation writes another chapter in this storybook, and the characters all have different motivations and points of view, but the principal causes of conflict remain the same.

On one side sits comfort and acceptance. On the other side sits fear and unfamiliarity. In between these simple concepts lies the Great Divide.

DELIVERANCE, '76

The old man's name was Edgar Bradford and he drove a red Chevy Vega. He used his little car to deliver newspapers, and the inside of his vehicle was a lot like the outside of its driver - messy and disheveled. Bundles of newspapers were always piled high on the seats, front and back, and Edgar never had any passengers as there simply wasn't any room for them. Even if there were, he lived alone, and Edgar was very much a loner.

Edgar's glasses were both thick in the frame and in the lens. His usual manner of dress consisted of blue work pants and long-sleeved, button-down shirts. Edgar's shoes were black in the boot and in the sole, and were well worn from shuffling through life.

Edgar's hair was once black as a young man, but as

an old man it had now turned gray, and there was more scalp showing than hair available to cover it. He began losing his hair at the center of his skull at the age of twenty-four, and each morning when he awoke and lifted his head off his flattened pillow he left a few more strands behind. By the age of sixty-one his hair was no more than an afterthought. A brush or comb was no longer required, and he merely used his hands to push the long wings from the side of his head up-and-over his naked crown. Edgar's hairstyle was a pushover, and so was Edgar the man.

Edgar took his job as a newspaper delivery man very seriously. He delivered papers throughout the town, starting as a fourteen year old delivery boy for the local newspaper, *The Minuteman Post. The Post* was a daily newspaper that covered the events and happenings of three neighboring towns and whose name originated after a once known but long forgotten figure in American history: the Town Crier.

The role of the Town Crier originated in Greek and Roman times, but their practices transcended time and rule, and the Anglican name was adopted by the

English in the 11th Century. Town Criers spread news to the masses and they spoke directly for the king. As Britain colonized the world, Town Criers eventually came to the Americas, and they were important players in governing, for there were few printing presses available, and the populace was mostly illiterate. Criers stationed themselves in front of squares, marketplaces, and inns and called the citizens to listen for the latest news, often by ringing a bell to gather a crowd and by shouting their words in loud, boisterous tones. After orating the news they nailed their announcement to a nearby wall or door and "posted their notice" for the educated townsfolk to read at their convenience. Edgar was his town's Crier, and he left his *Post* at the door of each citizen.

At age fourteen he pedaled his bicycle to deliver papers along his route in the afternoons, starting with the shuttered Colonial style homes on Main Street. Many bore wooden plaques by their front door that identified them as members of the Historical Society - a coveted mark that distinguished one old home as more significant than the average, ordinary old home.

He then circled back on Thurston Street, past the town cemetery (and home to the town's founding fathers) and all the way to The Glenview - the brick built nursing home that sat at his route's end. It wasn't an overly ambitious route, fifty-five papers on his busiest day, but it was his and it was only the beginning.

By the time Edgar turned seventeen he had quit school. He was left to his own devices as a child so that as a young man a job was worth more to him than an education. He expanded his route of *The Post* to include two hundred homes and picked up the route for the much larger regional paper, *The Globe*, which he delivered to two hundred and fifty homes and businesses each weekday morning, and two hundred and eighty every Sunday morning. Edgar was a hard worker, but he was content to deliver papers for a living and content to live in the same house and in the same town.

As an old man he still began his day by lifting his head up off his flattened pillow at four in the morning, getting dressed, and backing his Chevy Vega up to the top of his driveway where the delivery truck dumped the bundles of papers. He lifted each bundle, fifty papers per, by the string that held them together and loaded them into the Vega's trunk and onto the seats.

Edgar held a monopoly on *The Post* and *The Globe* as, over time, he acquired route after route, outlasting every paper boy and girl, usurping and adding to his territory until he laid claim to all routes in town for both publications. From the original route on Main Street in the town's center to the most rural outskirts in the salt-marsh, where homes were built on stilts and sat surrounded by patches of red and pink sea lavender, it was all his. The only folks who didn't receive a paper from the hand of Edgar were those who didn't want one. But for a man so vital and prevalent about town, Edgar was largely invisible.

His job began long before most people woke, and even though he spent the day driving about town in his red, rusty Vega, they only caught a glimpse of the man as he passed by, arm cocked with paper in hand. Edgar was no mystery since a mystery requires a party who wants to know something more. Nobody wanted to know Edgar, and Edgar was content to remain unknown. He did not attend town meetings or church services, and he only ventured out to buy groceries at the market, and for breakfast every Sunday morning at the Wamesit Diner – only after *The Globe's* Sunday edition was delivered of course.

While they did not know the man, they certainly knew his work. When the town discovered the "War to end all Wars" had begun and ended, Edgar literally gave them the news. When the town lost its first son in the war that followed nearly thirty years later, Edgar put it on their doorsteps and in their mailboxes. "*Prohibition Repealed*," "*Roosevelt Touts New Deal*," "*Man Walks on Moon*," and "*Ford Pardons Nixon*" were just some of the headlines hastily grabbed by Edgar and neatly folded, wrapped tight with a rubber band, and then tossed (never recklessly but always with purpose) for the subscriber to discover.

The Crier's reign came to an end on Sunday, July 4, 1976. When Edgar's neighbor opened his door to retrieve his morning paper, he paused and looked around in disbelief. *The Globe* was always on his front steps waiting for him. "Where is my paper?" he muttered.

The neighbor slowly walked down his front steps and up the stone walkway in his slippers and pajamas, under cover of a loosely tied and frayed bathrobe. He hesitated, wary of being seen outside in his morning dress. He glanced around in hopes of finding his paper under a shrub or tucked inside of his mailbox. He needed to satisfy his need for news, and when he reached the sidewalk that connected his yard to the neighbor he knew only as "the guy who delivers papers," he caught a glimpse of something sticking out beyond the tired white picket fence that separated their two properties. Squinting in the morning light, he focused and realized that he was staring at the bottom of a pair of worn out shoes.

Edgar's body lay at the top of his own driveway, surrounded by bundles of *The Globe* morning edition, all with the headline, "*Happy 200th America!*" printed above the fold.

Edgar Bradford died as he lived - alone and with his newspapers. Edgar's Vega sat idling above him, with a full tank of gas and with the hatchback wide open, patiently waiting to receive the day's delivery.

The paper route would live forever, but the Town Crier was now dead.

Edgar's body was claimed by a relative, and the man did so more out of obligation than anything else. Over the course of his life Edgar had planned for the deliverance of the news and little else. There was only a simple graveside service and a few flowers placed on the stubby non-descript granite marker that lay above the fold of earth.

Many times seemingly unremarkable people lead very remarkable lives. This was the case for Edgar Bradford - whose life was dedicated to his town and to the news that happened in and around it.

But Edgar's life and his death went unnoticed and without so much as a post.

THE SPAN OF A BRIDGE, '77

There's a place out on the edge of town, where the marsh-land lies between solid earth and the mighty Atlantic, and helps keep the coastal winds and waters at bay, and where, upland, Marsh Hill Lane peels off Main Street and heads in that direction. At the road's furthest point, where the cottages are small and nestled among the whispering pines is a place protected from time and preserved by memory.

Marsh Hill Lane fades into a rutted parking lot formed of a mixture of packed dirt and bits of crushed white shells. Behind and to the right of the parking lot is the outer edge of the town's dark forest, and to the left is the great salt marsh and the river that runs through it. Sloping down into the river is the town's Landing – a paved ramp where pickup trucks back their boat trailer down into the water until their wheels lie submerged, and the boats are released into, or pulled out of, the river. River access is only open to residents of the town, and although trespassers never receive a fine like the sign next to the ramp suggests, they can suffer something much harder to take - the wrath of the locals.

On the far side of the parking lot, along the river's edge and surrounded by the tallest of grasses and reeds is Smitty's Marina. Smitty is a country gentleman with very deep (and very tight) pockets, and his wooden shingle sided building is stained a faded gray with equally faded black and crooked louvered shutters that framed his windows. A rusted red and white metal sign with holes from a scattered buckshot round nailed next to the front door proclaims "Live Bait!" Smitty sells copies of *The Minuteman Post*, penny candy, homemade slices of pie, and cans of tonic. He also repairs and stores boats for the locals year-round.

A wooden planked pier stretches from the store's front porch out to the river, and a fueling station and fresh water hose is available for his customers at its end. Smitty also owns a string of floating wooden docks along the river's edge, each connected by a series of gang planks to the shoreline. People pay a handsome price to dock their boats at Smitty's during the summer months, and he feels no sorrow for squeezing it out of them.

Fishermen and pleasure boaters launch, dock, and refuel in this busy but tranquil setting…and as they make their way along the river, heading to and from the open ocean, they pass through the great salt marsh and beneath a box beam railroad bridge.

The box beam is a simple bridge, and it bears heavy loads by using triangles at the core of its design. Each side of the bridge is made of hardened steel beams with angled, alternating triangles, one pointing up then one pointing down, and the individual beams are all joined together by massive rivets. The girders of this particular box beam bridge were cast in the fiery furnaces of a Youngstown metal yard, shortly after the men who worked it came home from Korea. The beams were transported from Ohio and were assembled on site, and the bridge was built upon three bases - enormous granite slabs piled upon one another and designed to withstand the weight of the trains and the current of water that flows around them

The bridge was assembled for the purpose of threading passengers and freight across the river, at a point just over a mile before it opens up and spills out into The Sound. It spans a narrow but deep and gentle bend, where the dry-land ends and the great salt marsh begins. The river that flows beneath the bridge makes its way down from the highlands, and by the time it reaches the bridge its fresh water contents have blended with the salty sea water drawn in from the ocean. On each side, buried deep into the river's muddy banks and reaching all the way up to the main cross beam of the bridge is a marker, measured in feet, showing boaters how much clearance is made available by the tides.

The great salt marsh that surrounds this crooked and meandering estuary defines and guides the river and seeks its level at the instruction of the tides – gratefully absorbing the tidal overflow and then trustingly yielding it back. At all times the marsh land's fauna and mudflats are teeming with life, seen and unseen - life that depends upon the massive network of sturdy, green, and sometimes flattened cord grass. Combined, the marsh grasses form one of the world's largest living organisms and serves as a buffer, a filter, and a sanctuary. Its dead and decaying matter serve as an abundant food source for the smallest of organisms – serving up the first course in nature's food chain for marine fish and shellfish.

During high tide, the lower marsh grasses bend with the water and the breeze. At low tide, the rich muddy bottom of the upper marsh is left to dry out in the sun and lies dotted with shallow pools of green, nutrient rich water that teems with minnows and the muddy footprint of a stalking Great Blue. The scope of the marsh is enormous - it spans thousands of acres, and as one travels downriver and slips out from under the other side of the railroad bridge the great marsh unfolds and fills the horizon for as far as the eye can see. Just beyond your sight line, if you were to follow the quiet river to its end, you would find the angry and rolling waters of the Atlantic.

To seek out and find this particular landscape today

is to find it as it once was. The end of Marsh Hill Road remains relatively unchanged. The river water still laps at the wooden posts of Smitty's pier, the air remains thick from the salty sea and hydrogen sulfide gas of the mudflats, and the drivers seek the shady parking spot for their pick-up truck and empty trailer. The seemingly endless waves of green cord grass surround the ribbon of blue river water as it snakes its way through, and as the river bends gently, the rusted box beam railroad bridge stands front and center...

...Vincent Eldridge lived in a simple house – a converted summer cottage originally constructed at the time of the Nation's happy days. It sat at the edge of the dry-land and happened to be the very last house on Marsh Hill Lane. From his corner bedroom window Vincent could see through the thinning trees and catch a glimpse of the great salt marsh and the railroad tracks. While he knew the tracks crossed the river and ran somewhere north and south, he didn't know much more than that. Nor did he have any inclination to find out.

Vincent Eldridge was awkward, and like his name

nothing about him seemed to flow very well. He was a fantastically unremarkable dresser and his dark hair was forced to part in the middle when it really wanted to go to one side. The truth be told, Vincent was uncomfortable in his own skin - a tough affliction for anyone but none greater than a seventeen year old boy. He spent more time trying to blend in with his surroundings than to chance standing out by any measure, and as a result Vincent rarely took a risk.

A dream unfulfilled makes for a sad story; a dream never dreamt makes for something worse. Vincent spent his time biding his time, with no plan and no goal, and yet (and this is the tragedy) he was always waiting for something to happen – that moment when his life would change. It seemed to Vincent as if that moment would never happen. Until one day he got lucky, and like most things Vincent never saw it coming.

On that day he grabbed his lucky pocket knife off his dresser, and on his way out the front door he stooped to pick up his tackle box and fishing pole. The tide was high and the morning train had just passed by so he knew the tracks were safe for walking. As he left the shade of his screened in front porch and stepped out from under the giant pine and past a crowded bed of orange tiger lilies, Vincent felt the warmth of the early summer sun. His final school year was in the books, and he had decided to make good use of his day of freedom by fishing on the other side of the river, where the summer rentals sat high on their stilts out in the marsh. The worms he purchased at Smitty's last weekend were languishing, but they still had enough wriggle left in them to do the job.

He walked his way down towards the end of Marsh Hill Lane until he came to the point where the railroad tracks – which until then ran parallel with the road – veered off to the left as they headed out and over the marsh. He climbed through the brush and thickets and up to the track bed and began walking towards the river. He had made this trek countless times over the years, and as a young boy he would have to step and hop to match his strides with the spacing of the railroad ties. He noticed how the thick ties and stones spread between them were grimy and dirty - the result of the powerful locomotives and all their machinations and lubrications.

Vincent was also aware that, as a young man, his gate matched the ties' spacing perfectly, and because of that, his stride was natural and comfortable. But deep inside he couldn't help but realize that there would come a time, and he knew it would be very soon, when fishing and walking the tracks would not be so natural for someone his age. So, he kept his head down, paid close attention to each step, and enjoyed the comfort of the moment.

The trees that lined the tracks began to melt away and were gradually replaced by the brush and grass that had taken root in the sea sediments of the upper marsh. The box beam railroad bridge came into Vincent's full view, and in the background sat Smitty's Landing - the parking lot full of Chevrolet and Ford pick-up trucks with their empty trailers, indicating the ocean was a busy place. On the other side of the bridge, Vincent could see the summer cottages and a lone figure walking the tracks in his direction.

He hoped it wasn't one of the Racket boys. Jason

and Kenny Racket were a constant thorn in Vincent's side and had been for most of his life. They lived up on Main Street and ventured down to the marsh to roam and do what they pleased. If they felt like fishing it was not uncommon for them persuade Vincent to surrender his pole to them and use up all his worms.

Vincent looked back down at his shoe-tops and began to ponder a way out of such a predicament, despite knowing the outcome was destined to play itself out the same way it had dozens of times before. He was no more than a hundred yards from passing under the first beam of the rusty rivet riddled bridge, when he realized it wasn't a Racket boy at all. It was a girl. That was the moment that Vincent cast his eyes on Lacey O'Brien's for the first time.

Lacey had come up from the Valley to spend the summer with her dad. He taught a coastal soil erosion course at the college and rented one of the stilt cottages out in the marsh so he could extend his already endless studies and papers, and the setting made for a perfect laboratory. Many years before, when Lacey's mother realized she was an afterthought instead of a wife, she left the botanist and her daughter. But Lacey was strong and never saw her parents' problems as her own. She was sixteen in years but older and wiser than that.

She blew onto the scene like a high pressure system coming in from the North Atlantic. She did not suffer fools and said what was on her mind and said it without hesitation. More often than not she was right in what she said. When Lacey chartered a course she used her brains and determination to get to where she wanted to be and she almost always navigated her way there. But she wasn't just the smartest or most dogged person in a room. Lacey's thick, shoulder length blonde hair was naturally curled tight, her eyes flashed blue or green (depending on the color clothing she wore), and her full cheeks tinged of blush when temperatures or temper flared. On one cheek, much to her dismay, was the slightest imperfection (hence her dismay) - a birthmark. Lacey O'Brien was the entire package, and she was literally heading on a track towards an unaware and unsuspecting Vincent.

The two strangers continued on towards one

another until they stood face to face in the middle of the box beam bridge. Lacey, never at a loss for words or nerve, initiated. "Hi. I'm Lacey. What are you trying to catch?"

"A fish," mumbled Vincent, looking at his shoe tops, hoping a limited engagement would send this girl on her way.

"Funny guy," said an amused Lacey. "I meant what *kind* of fish. I'm up here for the summer. Why don't you show me how to catch one. I might as well learn."

But before Vincent could reply, she held up her hand, simulating a stop sign and said, "I want no part of any worms. You do that for me." she instructed.

Vincent looked back over his shoulder, hoping one of the Racket boys would intervene.

"You know my name, now what's yours?"

Lacey had a crystal ball for a mind's eye - an ability to sense and see things before any tangible evidence presented itself – and in her mind's eye she saw something about this particular boy that was different from the others. Beneath Vincent's awkward exterior she sensed a person and potential that the boy himself did not know was there. She was intrigued, so she adjusted her course and set her sights on Vincent.

Vincent had a very different mind's eye. It was near sighted – focused mostly on the present and often stuck in the past. Choosing the path of least resistance, as he was apt to do, he surrendered his fishing pole to Lacey and said, "O.k." and they headed back towards Lacey's side of the river to fish, together.

That is how they spent their first day and how they spent their summer - together. But fishing was merely the vehicle, the safe excuse to get together. Vincent thought how lucky he was to have found someone who liked to land fish, while Lacey spent the summer trying to land Vincent.

They would meet early in the morning and fish for a while but would then leave their poles at Lacey's and spend their days in and around the marsh and river. They would often fill a brown paper bag with Swedish Fish and Nonpareils from Smitty's and set out in Vincent's skiff among the network of channels in the marsh. One evening after supper, Lacey and Vincent met at Smitty's for a slice of Mrs. Smitty's (that's how she was known) deep dish apple pie, and Lacey nearly fell off her stool laughing when an embarrassed Vincent accidently ordered "sheep dip apple pie." And on an August morning, when Kenny Racket reached out to grab Vincent's fishing pole, Lacey grabbed Kenny's arm and flipped him over her shoulder and then proceeded to yell, "That's right, you better run!" when Kenny turned tail and fled.

While their days were busy, their nights were quiet and spent mostly at a small plastic table with green table cloth on the deck of Lacey's cottage, sitting in the dark above the quiet marsh with a kerosene lantern, two cans of Fanta, and a deck of Bicycle cards. In the shelter and protection of the great marsh, Lacey and Vincent became friends. They used their time together to talk about their hopes and fears - their insecurities and their experiences. Yes, Lacey wanted much more from Vincent, but she waited, albeit impatiently, knowing that he was different and worth waiting for. She was not used to not getting what she wanted, but she was willing to settle for what she had - for the time being.

Vincent and his pocket knife had been inseparable since the day he received it as a present from his mom and dad on his 13th birthday. One morning, as he cut his line to thread a new hook for Lacey, he closed it up and handed it to her, looking her in the eye but without saying why. She pocketed it, understanding that it was a substantial gesture from a simple boy, and Lacey took his gesture to her heart.

But it was still not enough.

The summer ticked away and the evening before Lacey was due to return to the Valley, the two young adults lay in their respective beds staring at their respective ceilings. The summer was over and they were confronted with the end of their time together in the shelter of the great marsh. True to their form, the high pressure system that was Lacey lay angry about her reality and her lack of control over it. The low pressure system that was Vincent lay sad, but resigned. He pondered the impossible "How's?" and "What if's?" while Lacey plotted the "How-to" and the "When's?"

Unable to bear it any longer, Lacey kicked off her

sheet, clicked the fan on her nightstand to "High" (to mask the creaky wooden floor), slipped on her sneakers and snuck out into the night. She made her way down the wooden steps of her cottage and out on to the floating boardwalk that led to the dirt road. As she did all summer long, she hiked the railroad bed in the direction of the box beam railroad bridge, but this time she was not going to meet Vincent. As Lacey strode to the very center of the bridge - the spot where she set her sights upon Vincent for the first time – the blue moon cast a silvery hue upon the marsh and reflected brightly in the black and swollen river.

Turning her back toward Vincent's house she pulled out his pocket knife and dropped to one knee and set to work, etching into the railroad tie what she knew from the first day they met, but what Vincent still needed help realizing. Beneath the layer of grime and under the layer of tar sealant the sharp blade exposed the timber's freshly preserved wood, still light in color and deep in contrast to all the blackness that surrounded it. Using a combination of the pointed tip and the long sharp edge of the blade, Lacey carved in large stick-like letters her own initials, followed by Vincent's, in an age-old declaration that spanned generations.

Lacey knew that Vincent Eldridge would never look up and see it for himself, so she put it right where he would find it. She had to spell it out for Vincent: "L.O. + V.E."

At eight o'clock the next morning, Vincent heard the steel wheels of the morning train singing their metallic song. It was time to meet Lacey, so he grabbed his fishing pole and his tackle box and set out for their final morning of fishing. Lacey had already left her cottage, but she left her pole behind. They walked the tracks toward one another, each at their own pace. Lacey walked deliberately at what lay ahead while Vincent walked cautiously, looking down at what was.

The late summer's sun had just begun to burn through the morning haze, and shafts of sunlight streamed down upon the field of green and river of blue. Lacey shielded the sun from her eyes and watched Vincent as he looked down upon his measured steps, unaware of her gaze.

The two summer companions were making their way towards one another in the setting of the great salt marsh. Two friends brought together by the span of a bridge.

AFTER THE STORM PASSED, '78

"This storm will be measured in feet, not inches. Expect the snow to start falling shortly after seven o'clock this morning," said the crackled voice of WBZ meteorologist Don Kent over the radio.

Dad kept the radio on top of the refrigerator so that nobody would change the station on him. He liked to listen to the news, especially the weather, before heading off to work in the morning. It was six-thirty and we were all in the kitchen, having our breakfast and looking out the window for the first sign of snowflakes.

"Oh that's not what they said on Channel Five last night. They said it was going to make a mess of the day but wouldn't be more than eight to ten inches in total," said my mom as she eyeballed a scoop of Brim instant coffee. Dad was a mechanic and he liked to be in the shop by eight, so she only brewed fresh coffee on weekend mornings, when they had more time to enjoy it.

Mom had her back turned to us and was slipping Dad a decaffeinated brand, because according to mom, "He needed to relax a little."

Dad snapped his head away from his oatmeal and defiantly defended the man whose voice gave us the weather forecast each day. "Don Kent is the only one who gets it right, Shirley!"

Afraid that everyone in the kitchen still did not believe him, he continued. "Don Kent knows what he's talking about," and raising his spoon into the air to punctuate his editorial, he finished with, "The rest of them are just guessin'!"

My sisters looked up from their cereal with quiet curiosity as a glob of oatmeal dribbled down from my father's spoon and onto the cuff of his oil stained work shirt.

Mom raised a skeptical eyebrow and placed the steaming coffee cup in front of him. Using a dish towel to wipe his cuff clean of the unnoticed oatmeal, she shared her own thoughts on the matter. "Well, Don Kent isn't driving to his shop today - you are. So please be careful."

"I'm closin' early. Don Kent doesn't exaggerate so I'm comin' home after lunch," Dad continued, beating the dead horse a little more.

How many times was he going to say Don Kent?

I was in a particularly good mood that Monday morning. It was February 6th in the year 1978, and I was fifteen years old. School was cancelled for the day because of the impending storm, and I found myself hoping Dad's strange allegiance to Don Kent was well founded. If so, I might be looking at another day off tomorrow. At age fifteen it was all about me.

Dad left for work, my little sisters did some baking with my mom, and I went outside with my friends, and it snowed – all day and all night, and all the next day, too. For thirty six hours it was an onslaught of what Dad called, "Biblical proportions," and by the time Tuesday evening rolled around most of New England was buried under ridiculous amounts of snow - no less than two feet and some areas by as much as four feet.

The Blizzard of '78 snuck up on everybody - except Don Kent and his loyal disciples.

Looking back, when I think about how it snowed non-stop for nearly two days, it still seems pretty incredible. I can say with certainty that I've never experienced anything like it since. During the heart of the storm it snowed as much as four inches in an hour, and hurricane force winds blew upwards of 80 miles per hour. It wreaked havoc, trapping and burying cars on Route 128 as people tried to make their way home from work, blew drifts of snow fifteen feet high, and rendered roads impassable for days. But don't be fooled by my nostalgia. Twenty-nine people lost their lives in my state alone.

My town was on the coast, where high tide came and went four times during this particular prolonged storm and joined forces with the full moon to sweep summer homes out into the Atlantic Ocean. In other coastal communities, people's homes with all their earthly possessions were ripped out to sea or battered to splinters.

Some people were asphyxiated in their stranded

cars when their idling vehicles, left running for hours at a time for warmth, became buried under the snow and the exhaust fumes wound up being recycled into the car's airflow. People gave up trying to remove the snow from their driveways or uncover their cars because they simply couldn't keep up with the pace at which the falling snow came down, or they simply ran out of room to shovel or plow. We just hunkered down in our homes until it stopped.

All of New England surrendered to the elements - for nearly a week when it was all said and done. The Blizzard of 1978 changed lives and landscapes forever, and that's why the people who lived through it still talk about it today - including me.

My house looked out at the center of town, where Main Street was intersected on opposite sides by Cross and Church Streets, and its traffic flow was regulated by the only signal light around for miles. It was a small town, but a busy one, and I liked living in the middle of things. The white Congregational Church with its pointed steeple that housed a bell and enormous clock sat on one corner of the intersection, and a stone-wall where The Trouble Kids hung out in the summer wrapped itself around other.

It was now early Tuesday evening, and while the fury of the storm had subsided, the snow still blew in swirling white currents and showed no sign of letting up. Darkness had set in, and the smell of mom's pot-roast filled the downstairs. I knelt on the couch in my living room and looked out the window that faced the intersection, waiting for something to happen.

The traffic light was blinking a malfunctioning yellow, and all the sharp angles and edges of Main Street were softened by the thick coating of white. Every time a heavy plow had cleared a path, Mother Nature covered it up again with a gust of wind and another layer of snow. The road was clogged and impassable, but snowmobiles had buzzed through earlier and their sound had drawn me to the window. They had long since sped off into the night.

The room was dark, and the draft from the window sill chilled my arms.

If I was in a good mood on Monday and Tuesday morning when I found out school was canceled, I was in a glorious mood when the Governor declared a state of emergency, ordered all vehicles off the road, called in the National Guard to help clear the streets, and declared schools across the state closed for the remainder of the week.

I could hardly believe how lucky I was, and my mind turned to all the things I would do for myself and with my friends - and all the homework I wouldn't have to see or do over the next several days. Sitting there in the dark, my immediate future looked bright, and I was antsy for the fun to begin.

Dad's heavy steps thundered down the stairs and brought me back to the present. When he reached the main floor, he saw me staring out the window and sensed my state of mind. "Aren't you the lucky one? Mikey the Greek gave you a pardon, eh?"

Dad liked to categorize and give nicknames to people he wasn't fond of, and that included our Governor. "Well, good thing. There's lots of shoveling to be done." He grunted as he turned the corner and tracked the smells coming from the kitchen with his nose.

I pursed my lips but said nothing in reply. I watched him out of the corner of my eye and saw the outline of his bushy beard and large frame as it filled the doorway and crossed into the light of the kitchen.

Dad could be a hard man to have for a father. He never let me enjoy the moment and made me spend my precious hours doing things that I did not want to do. I liked to daydream, and I swear he never did that once.

All he cares about is work, work, and more work. What about me? I let out a sigh that steamed up the frosty pane in front of me.

I was aware of my parents' voices coming from the kitchen, but I wasn't paying attention to what they were saying until my Dad's booming voice cut into me.

"Scotty. Get your long-johns on and get dressed for outside. Put your bread bags over your socks before you get in your boots. You'll wanna keep your feet dry."

Are you kidding me! I yelled to myself. I glanced at the clock on the wall and it said five thirty. *We eat supper at six. What's he trying to prove?*

I lumbered upstairs and got dressed, all the while thinking about how I would rather stay inside than shovel snow. When I came back down, Dad was waiting for me, all ready to go.

He looked bigger than ever, all layered up and wrapped in his giant flannel coat and matching knit hat. Even his beard looked fuller as the scarf around his neck pushed it out.

"Dinner will be plenty hot when you get back," said my sympathetic Mom as I finished gearing up for the elements.

"Get back?" I asked, trying to keep my balance while hopping and pulling on a boot, all in one motion. "I thought we were shoveling?"

"You are," stated Dad. "But first, we walk." He was a man of few words but the words he did say left nothing unsaid. Dad stooped down and scooped up a picnic basket. My annoyance gave way to confusion, but my instinct for survival suppressed any further questions.

Mom put her hands on my shoulders and leaned in for a kiss good-bye from both of us. The door in the kitchen led to our garage and out to our driveway. The air inside the garage was cold on my face, but it was still and quiet. Dad leaned over and lifted up the garage door. As it clattered up and over us, I couldn't believe what I saw on the other side. A cross-section of snowdrift as tall as me was staring back at us.

We both paused.

This is good. Maybe he realizes how stupid this is and we can go back inside.

"Use the side door. The wind gets cut down over there. The drifting shouldn't be as bad," said Dad. He reached up high and pulled the door back down. "Grab your shovel." Then he pulled opened the door.

Dad was right, and I was screwed. The snow was only up to his knees.

"Let's make our way out to Main Street and then up Cross."

"Why are we going up Cross Street?" I winced, waiting for a tongue lashing that never came. Cross Street was a long, dead end road that came out on the other side of the church. There was the fire station and a series of simple homes but nothing else. We didn't even have good friends up there. It was mostly old people.

"Hold your shovel up high so it doesn't drag. It'll only make it harder to keep up with me," he said, ignoring my question and exploding into the snow bank.

We bullied our way down and out the driveway – me armed with my shovel and my dad with his picnic basket. I followed his footsteps, trudging along behind him. Main Street was not nearly as snow covered as our driveway. The town plows had put up a decent fight before surrendering. We walked until we stood at the intersection - the very place that just a short time ago I was looking at from the living room window.

It was a surreal moment – standing there in the dark and among the falling snow. Mom was always worried about us crossing this busy intersection, and yet there we were, just me and my dad, standing smack in the center and under the blinking yellow traffic light.

I looked up into the night. I wanted to stand there some more - to think about things and enjoy the moment a little longer. I never had the chance to look closely at my house from here, and it looked so small to me now with just the yellow hue of our lights in the windows and its flat-angled roof all covered in snow and wrapped in blackness. The pillared church was now directly in front of us, and the steeple continuously materialized and faded out of focus in the swirling snow. The blackened circle of the clock face was barely visible, and the weathervane that I knew was at the top had disappeared into the shadowy heavens.

Dad's figure interrupted me as he cut in front of my sight-line. Snow decorated his beard and he breathed heavily from the effort it required for us to get there.

"C'mon. Let's walk in the snowmobile tracks. It'll make it easier," he said, looking down at me.

What I wouldn't give for a snowmobile right now. I'd pick up Jamie and we'd cruise all over town, going over jumps and tearing past all our friends' houses.

Instead, we turned up Cross Street, made our way along the broadside of the Church and beyond the fire station, and then further down the dark and quiet street. Our boot prints disturbed the pattern of the snowmobile tracks that were revealed to us only by the periodic streetlight.

"Dad?..."

"What?"

"Why do you have a picnic basket? Are we going to eat something? I'm hungry."

"Not everything is about you. C'mon. Let's go see Mrs. Knowles."

Mrs. Knowles lived in the first house on the left hand side of the street after the fire station. She was an old woman, and I knew her husband had died a long time ago and that she lived alone. I'd see her when I'd ride my bike up and down the street, and in the summer she usually wore a house dress and had curlers in her hair while she swept her driveway. That always struck me as funny - the act of sweeping your driveway. I never had the inclination to sweep my kitchen floor, never mind my driveway.

Dad put the basket down and rang Mrs. Knowles' doorbell and made circular "get busy" motions with his other hand. "Clean off the steps and her walkway. She'll tell you not to, but don't stop. Just tell her, "it's not a bother.' "

"Butch! What are you doing out in this? Is everything all-right?" I found that funny too - Mrs. Knowles calling my dad "Butch". That's what the guys at the shop and his close friends called him, not the old ladies from church - or so I thought. She stood in the open doorway in her housedress and bathrobe with curlers in her hair.

Does she ever take those out?

"Oh everything's fine, Mrs. Knowles."

I found it equally amusing that Dad was so formal.

"We were just checking to see if you needed anything. Shirley made some banana bread with the girls yesterday, and she wanted to make sure you had something to eat. The roads won't be cleared for quite some time so this will tide you over should you want a little snack." Dad reached down into the picnic basket and pulled out a package wrapped tightly in foil.

"Hope you like it," he said handing it over to her.

My shovel scraped the cement walkway and Mrs. Knowles looked down from her front steps at me. "Hi there, Scotty. Don't you worry at all about me. I can shovel that myself. You save your strength for sledding."

"Oh, it's not a bother," I replied, glancing at my dad who was nodding in agreement at my scripted response.

Dad told Mrs. Knowles we could not come inside to warm up and that we had to get back home and thanked her for the offer. He also reminded her that her car's inspection sticker was due to expire at the end of the month and for her to bring it in so he could check it over for her and get it taken care of. Mrs. Knowles said she would. Dad watched me finish shoveling.

"Now to the Shea's."

Mrs. Shea was nice enough, but Mr. Shea was a grumpy old man. He didn't like people on his lawn, and it had the perfect natural jump for our bikes. His house was set back off the road, and a drainage ditch that ran alongside his driveway served as a perfect launching spot for us. The only trouble was that his perfectly manicured lawn served as the only landing spot.

If Mr. Shea was home, he'd yell, "Get off my grass!" My friends and I would each get one chance to jump, and then we would pedal like hell down the street so he could not identify us. The only advantage we had was that Mr. Shea had a left shoe with an extra six inches of sole to compensate for one leg being shorter than the other. He hobbled around with the one heavy shoe and smoked cigarettes all the time, and as far as I knew he never knew it was me who was jumping on to his grass…I hoped.

"Butchy! What are you doing out on a night like this? C'mon in before you catch cold. I'll have Evelyn put on some coffee for you."

"Hey, Tom. No, no. I'm good, thanks. Shirley has been putting the clamps on my caffeine intake - claims she can tell when I'm too wired up. We're just checking in to make sure you're all set. How are things? Quite a storm isn't it?"

"It's a doozy for sure. Boy did they get this one wrong. They said it was supposed to be just under a foot."

I could feel my father fighting the urge to introduce

Mr. Shea to Don Kent, but instead he deflected the conversation and they began to talk about the Bruins and their Stanley Cup chances.

I stopped shoveling and stared up at them in wonder. Two of the hardest people I knew were chatting and making small talk like Mom did with the other moms at the grocery store.

Dad was standing at the top of Mr. Shea's concrete steps and noticed my pause and glanced down at me. His raised eyebrows asked, "And you stopped shoveling why?"

I quickly resumed my work, and as I pitched the snow aside in a pile I saw Dad reach into the picnic basket and hand Mr. Shea a pack of cigarettes. "Take these in case you run out. I know they aren't your brand but it's better than nothing. I don't think we'll be able to get to the store for a couple of days at least."

"Alright Butchy - will do. Thanks a lot," said Mr. Shea, pocketing a pack of my dad's Rothman's and turning his attention to me as my shovel scraped his walkway.

Here it comes. He's going to remember me and my bike jumps and let me have it, and then Dad's gonna' do the same.

My stomach tensed up, and I pretended I was too concerned about the quality of my shoveling to notice Mr. Shea - but I could hear him as he shifted his balance and dragged his heavy shoe down on to the front steps and leaned out over the railing to get a better look at me.

"That's your boy? He's gotten so big. I remember when he was just a little guy, riding around his big-wheel in your driveway. He's changed so much. I wouldn't even recognize him if he rode past me on the street."

"Mmmm. He's still got some growing to do," said my dad. "Keep shoveling son."

After the Shea's we walked to several more houses, zig-zagging Cross Street as we went. At each house Dad made a delivery in one form or another. He dropped off mom's homemade preserves for Mrs. Bailey, a recipe for Mrs. Dodd, lit the furnace pilot which had gone out at the Merry's, and delivered a 4-pack of Natural Light beer cans to the Robinson brothers. At each of these stops I shoveled their walkway and steps. When we reached the last house on the street, my arms were limp and fingers frozen, and my empty stomach yearned for Mom's pot roast.

"It's nearly eight o'clock. Let's head home," said Dad, glancing at his watch. He actually sounded disappointed.

We walked for a while, tracing our route back. I was too tired to talk and didn't have too much to say anyway. This was not how I wanted to spend my evening - shoveling steps for old people. We backtracked, and as we passed each house we had stopped at along the way. I looked at all the work I had done and noticed it was slowly being reclaimed by the falling snow.

What was this all about?

As we neared the backside of the Congregational Church, my dad pointed at a mountain of snow that the plows and front end loaders had deposited. It was pushed and piled all around a telephone pole that held a street light.

"Give me the shovel," he said, and he put down his

basket and took it from my hand before I even had a chance to pass it to him. Dad then proceeded to dig out two small egg-shaped caves in the mound, and when he was finished he stabbed the shovel in the snow and motioned toward one and commanded, "Take a seat."

My dad threw himself down in one with gusto, as if he was the one who had done all the shoveling. Out of his flannel coat pocket Dad pulled a can of Natural Light. In one quick motion he hooked his finger through the eyehole of the metal tab and ripped it off the can. The two of us sat in the snow under the glow of the streetlight, in silence.

As he tipped his head back and took a sip from the can I tipped my head back and looked up into the night. Giant snowflakes fell gently onto my eyelids and caused me to blink. The soft glow of the street light made it seem as if we were on the inside of a recently shaken snow-globe.

Just then I realized how quiet the night was – there were no cars on the road or people about. No birds were singing and the wind had fallen off completely.

Dad and I were the only two souls out. It felt like we had the town to ourselves.

"Thanks for all the hard work tonight, Scotty," said Dad. He turned, and it seemed as if he were searching my eyes for recognition.

"You're welcome," I said, unsure of what else he wanted to hear. I broke eye contact and looked down at my snow boots.

"These folks are our neighbors, and it's our job to look out for one another, ya' know?" he said, throwing his head back and taking a long swig of his beer.

"Uh-huh." I uttered, still unsure of what I was supposed to say.

Dad continued. "There's always work to be done, and I try to help people out when I can, especially when God's pissed, like he is now," he said, gesturing with a fist-full of beer can to the walls of snow that lined the street in front of us. "Sometimes people just like to be reminded that they are not forgotten."

Dad looked off into the nothingness, as if he was chewing on his words a little more, and then he lifted the can back up to his mouth to wash them down. The hairs of his beard and mustache were wild and scraggly and full of snowflakes and frozen moisture beads from his breath. He took another long sip from the can and let out a loud, satisfied, "Ahhhhhhh."

Then he leaned over and held the beer in front of me and said, "Go ahead. Have a sip, but don't tell yer mother."

The edge of the can tasted like metal, and the beer like something worse. I filled my mouth with the slushy, bubbly liquid and swallowed it before I had a chance to think about what it would taste like going down. I grimaced and gave the can back to my dad, and he finished the rest.

"That pot roast is gonna taste good," he said, and he threw the empty can into the picnic basket and popped up on to his feet. I agreed about the pot roast, but was too tired to stand up and finish the trip home through the snow.

The church bell above us let loose the first of eight methodical rings. It shattered the stillness of the moment and appeared to prompt my Dad into action. He held out his hand and said, "C'mon. Let's go home."

I reached out and took his offering. His massive form easily pulled me up from my seat of snow and on to my feet. I couldn't help but notice how his fur-lined leather glove dwarfed my own hand.

There was a brief and awkward moment where my Dad did not release, and as we turned and slogged our way back through the snow covered street we held hands.

We walked side by side to the end of Cross Street and under the blinking yellow light of Main Street. As we passed back in front of the church and its towering pillars Dad gave a nod toward the building, as if it were part of our conversation. He said with a chuckle, "Damn. Don Kent really nailed it."

The vibrations from the church bell's eighth and final ring struggled to hang in the air with the snowflakes. I think it was the beer that made me feel warm inside.

THE OLD NEIGHBORHOOD, '79

Kathryn Bailey stood inside the foyer of her house. One hand leaned on her cane with the brim of a green woolen hat wedged between her forefinger and thumb, and the other hand pushed back the lace curtain from the looking glass of the front door.

Kathryn's matching green dress, garnished with a faux pearl necklace and earrings, while a bit dated in style, still looked its Sunday best, and if one looked closely at Kathryn's stockings their slight difference in shade would have revealed her failing vision.

She was waiting impatiently for her daughter. Ellen Bailey was Kathryn's ride to the ten o'clock church service, as she was every Sunday morning, and while Kathryn enjoyed the act of going to church, every so often - when the weather and timing were just right - Ellen would come by a little earlier to take Kathryn for a stroll through the old neighborhood.

Kathryn Bailey spent all eighty-two of her years in this small, New England town and the old neighborhood was a very special place within it.

"Hi Mom, sorry I'm late. I couldn't find my glasses again – seems to be happening all the time now. How are you feeling this morning?" asked Ellen, after finally pulling into the driveway and hurrying out of her car to help her mother down the front steps.

"I'm still breathing and taking nourishment," returned Kathryn, who had placed the hat on her head and was determinedly making her way past Ellen in the driveway, placing her cane ahead and then catching up to it with quick, choppy steps.

Kathryn's voice was pitched high and had a bit of a lilt. "We still have plenty of time. Just get my old chair and let's get going."

Kathryn liked to use the word "old" to describe anything that was familiar.

Ellen dutifully went inside Kathryn's foyer and wrestled with the collapsed wheelchair that lay against the steam radiator and lugged it back down the walkway. Using her key to open the trunk of her brown Ford Granada, she hoisted the chair and let it fall on top of the spare tire and slammed the trunk shut. After both ladies had settled into their seats, Ellen cautiously backed the car out of the driveway, and as she put it into gear and straightened out the Granada's wheels, any passer-by would have noticed how they cut similar profiles in the front seat.

It took only a few minutes for them to reach the church parking lot, which lay adjacent to the old neighborhood. The wheelchair made traveling the short distance between these two places a lot quicker for both women, and as Kathryn eased herself into the chair she reached a point where it was a lot easier to let gravity finish the job. Ellen steadied the push handles and looked at the lone blue station wagon parked beside the church's side entrance. "Looks like Marge came in a bit early today."

"Today's the family service, and she's setting up the children's choir," said the aged but ever alert Kathryn, laying her cane across her lap. "She's got them singing about insects and earthworms this morning. That won't go over well with the old folks."

"I'm sure it won't," smirked Ellen, who was now stooped over and fishing around to unlock the brake on her mother's chair. The old neighborhood was a mere block away, and the sloping sidewalk led them gently in that direction.

September was a few weeks old, and the morning air was caught between the coolness of the dewy grass and the warmth of the rising sun. The trees that lined the sidewalk around them were yellowing green, but an occasional branch showed a patch of bright red, as if the group of leaves could no longer bear the thought of the inevitable and made the collective choice to go on ahead of the others.

"Who do you want to visit today, Mom?" asked Ellen.

"Don't know, dear. Whoever happens to be awake this early," chuckled Kathryn.

Kathryn was contextually beautiful and always practical - as evidenced by the tissue sticking out of the cuff of her sleeve.

Her Sunday hat was pulled down low over her

thinning, white wispy hair, and its round woolen crest was decorated with a seasonal ribbon. Kathryn's face was creased and heavily wrinkled, and her skin was a pinkish white – a combination of her pale coloring and too much blush. Her lipstick was thickly applied and smudged – the result of her trembling hand.

Ellen pushed Kathryn in her chair as Kathryn had once pushed Ellen in a carriage. The daughter lovingly peeked around to make sure the morning sun was not in the mother's eyes. The child tucked a knitted afghan up and around the parent to help keep the chilly air at bay. Kathryn's life was very close to completing the full circle, and both women were well aware of that fact.

As they made their way, they chatted about the weather, wondered when the Edwards' were going to get around to painting their old house, and made comfortable small talk with one another. But as they turned through the wrought iron gates of the old neighborhood, their conversation tapered off and Ellen's grip on the wheelchair's push bars tightened - she sensed her mother was about to begin issuing directions. Ellen's instincts were right.

"Go down for a bit, until you get to the old Hale place," directed Kathryn.

The old neighborhood was an exclusive part of town, and when the residents moved in they almost never left. Each lot was symmetrical and their lawns were watered and manicured all summer long. Many had tasteful, colorful flower beds and an American flag planted out front. The old neighborhood was pure Americana - rich with history and heritage.

Daybreak was just a few hours old, and the old neighborhood was sleepy, with only Kathryn and Ellen up and about. As they made their way further up the narrow, winding road, Kathryn made up her mind about whom they were going to visit.

"Why don't we go see Eliza. Her place is just off to the right."

"Well I know where Eliza's is, Mom," stated Ellen, who always enjoyed their visits. Eliza had been Kathryn's friend since childhood, and she always gave her mother a reason to smile.

"Come on out my friend!" warbled Kathryn from

her wheelchair, leaning forward in anticipation. "Don't waste a beautiful day like this one. Winter is what's coming next, so you've got to take a day like this by the horns!"

Kathryn paused, thought for a moment, and then continued.

"Today makes me think of the time your dad took us out in the Plymouth that fall morning, out by old Minister's Woodlot, by the marshland. We were about nine or ten, and remember how that old road was full of potholes and bumps, and we were squeezed in together, bouncing up and down in the rumble seat 'til land's end.

"You were laughing so hard you made your dad pull over so that you could finish in the woods. Then old Charlie Jacobs came out of nowhere on his bicycle, just as you were coming out from behind that old tree with your dress all stuck up inside itself. The expression on his face made me laugh so hard that I wound up behind that old tree too."

Short of breath, Kathryn's voice struggled to maintain its volume, so she adjusted to a softer tone.

"For land's sake, we laughed all the way home, and all the while your daddy was shaking his head and muttering to himself, 'Three daughters and not one son.' Oh Lord, those were good times."

Kathryn let her thoughts and smile linger for another moment or two. "We have always been such good friends, you and I," she continued, talking to an absent Eliza.

Then she turned her head back to Ellen. "In my eighty-seven years I've met lots of people and made lots of acquaintances, but it's the friends – the true friends – that help carry you through life. We all hide a little bit of ourselves - put on a front or reveal only a little of what goes on up here," said Kathryn, pointing a bony finger to her temple.

"But your true friends are the ones you reveal your hopes and fears to…your dreams and your soul to."

Kathryn's voice trailed off, and she slowly moved her now fisted hand down to her left breast in a tender fashion. She continued, "Your friends are the ones who know you as well as you know yourself. Heck, sometimes they know you better."

Then, sinking back down in her wheelchair so that it appeared as if her shoulders were in a shrug position, she whispered, "Oh, how I wish you'd get up and come to church with us this morning."

"Let her be, Mom," suggested Ellen, who could sense a sadness creeping into her mother's voice. "We can come back another time. Who else would you like to visit?"

"Let's go stop in and see old Jack Brown. I haven't talked to Jack in a while."

Ellen tensed up. She didn't care for Jack Brown all that much, and the more she thought about how he checked out, leaving his wife and four kids, the more she felt she was justified in feeling that way. In her Christian mind the man was nothing more than a sinner, maybe a coward at best.

But Ellen didn't want to push her mother in any direction than the one that she wanted to go. So Ellen said nothing.

"I know what you're thinking, that old Jack Brown's a coward," chirped Kathryn as they approached his place. "Well, if old Jack came out right now I'd give the man a hug," she spat out.

"I always felt bad for old Jack. When you are lonely and desperate you sometimes lose hope, and when all hope is gone it is easy to give up. Old Jack has been sad since he was a child, and I always got the feeling that he sometimes just needed a hug. I don't think he ever got that many hugs as a little boy. Loneliness is a disease that can be cured. He just never got the medicine he needed. I'm old, and I don't know much, but I know that."

"Well, you can give him a hug if he's lucky enough to see you," said Ellen, wishing she could be as understanding. Looking at her watch, Ellen swung the chair to the left at the next cross-road. "Marge will be starting the intro in about fifteen minutes so let's swing down here and then head out. Who should we visit next?"

"How about old Doctor Bartlett?" said Kathryn. "I have something I would like to say to the man."

"Of course you do," replied Ellen.

As they continued on their path to the Bartlett place they waved to Chief Hardy, wondered what would have become of the Littlefield boy and badmouthed the politics of Walter Knowles when they passed his wife Elizabeth. While they failed to notice the town's newspaper delivery man, they snickered as they passed crotchety church deacon, Everett Faulkner, and agreed in modest, hushed tones about how handsome a man Sam White was.

Doctor Bartlett was at one time the town's only physician, and when he retired he had delivered more babies, diagnosed more cases of mumps, chicken pox, and pneumonia, set more casts and splints, and told more residents they were dying than any other doctor.

Doctor Bartlett had delivered Ellen into this world and also told John Bailey, Kathryn's husband of sixty one years, that he was going to die from the cancer that ravaged his body.

"Set me here so I can talk to him for a bit, sweetheart," said Kathryn, implying she wished to do so alone. "Why don't you go over and talk to the Gables girl."

"Okay Mom," said Ellen, surprised at her mother's affectionate tone. Kathryn was always a loving mother, but old yankees like Kathryn typically used proper nouns, not terms of endearment when addressing others.

Ellen took her time crossing the street and complimented Little Jennifer on her flowing blonde hair and noted how polite and perfectly mannered she was, and indicated that she looked forward to seeing her mother in church later in the morning.

Ellen glanced back at her mother and watched as her frail hand swept through the air as she spoke to the good Doctor. She waited a few minutes, and when her mother's arm lay still and propped over the arm of the wheelchair she said goodbye to Little Jennifer.

"How's Doctor Bartlett?" she asked, trying to sound casual, but sensing a heavy presence about her mother.

"Oh, he had no complaints," chuckled Kathryn. "I just thanked him for telling me the bone truth."

"What's the bone truth?" Ellen was an only child and she thought she had heard all of her mother's stories (she had, over and over again), but she was certain she had not heard this one.

"Oh, it's something old Doctor Bartlett told me two times in my life."

This sounded serious to Ellen, so she walked around to the front of her mother's chair and knelt down, putting one a hand on Kathryn's tired knee. "You never told me this before. What is the bone truth?"

"Well," said Kathryn, sharpening her focus on Ellen, "He said it when he put you in my arms, just seconds after you were born, and then he told me the same thing at your father's bedside when he passed. Both times, Doctor Bartlett looked me in the eye and said, 'Birth brings us great joy and death brings us great sorrow, but everything that happens in between is the bone truth."

As Kathryn spoke, she broke eye contact with Ellen and looked off into the early September sky, as if she were watching the two events unfold all over again.

"Well what on earth does that mean?" asked a confused Ellen, who liked to speak in more literal terms.

"I didn't quite know what it meant when you were

born. For lands sake, I was just a child myself at time. But I figured it out as time went by and when we lost your father it was plain as day. He meant that the act of being born and the act of dying aren't what define us – it's the experiences we have, the friends we make, and the people we love that are important. The life we lead is what makes that life complete.

"Those things are everlasting. So, when I find myself caught between a laugh and a tear, I just try to remember what old Doctor Bartlett told me. It gives me comfort and makes me look forward to living another day."

"Okay, Mom," said a somber Ellen. She patted her mother's knee and pushed herself back up and returned to the back of the wheelchair. "Let's get you inside the sanctuary without making too much of a distraction."

"Wait a minute. Let's go see your dad first. He's only a block away, and I don't need to say anything to him. He knows everything there is to know. Let's just give him a wave as we pass on by."

"Alright," said Ellen. "We'll drive by and give him a

wave then." With winter approaching, she knew there would not be many Sunday morning trips left to the old neighborhood with her mother, and it had been a while since Kathryn last visited John.

As they turned the corner and made their way past the other plots - the Proctors, the Jewetts, and the Todds, Ellen grimaced at the thought of what she was about to see.

The morning sun glinted off the chiseled marble marker that defined the boundary of her father's resting place.

She could easily read *John Bailey, 1895 – 1970*, and had come to accept her father's death, over time. It was the writing next to her father's that troubled her.

*Kathryn Bailey, 1897 – 19 *. Her mother's inevitable ending was spelled out for her to see and contemplate, and that was very difficult for Ellen. She paused a moment and looked down at the top of her mother's wide-brim hat. It nearly obscured Kathryn's slight body underneath.

Ellen would miss her terribly when she was gone. She could not imagine the feeling of loneliness her mother's death would bring to her, nor could she imagine a woman so full of life surrendering to the inevitable.

"I'm not afraid of dying, honey. I'm more afraid of not wanting to live anymore," said Kathryn, as if she knew what was passing through her daughter's mind at that very moment.

"I love you Mom," Ellen blurted out, clumsily.

"I love you too, Ellen. That's the bone truth."

Ellen and Kathryn made their way back under the yellowing shade willows and through the wrought iron fence to Main Street. The ringing church bell beckoned and their pace quickened.

Behind them, silently drifting in the current of the warm autumn air among the cold headstones, floated the experiences and the dreams (realized, broken, and abandoned) of the residents of the old neighborhood.

MY FRESH SHEET

I have discovered that I have the ability to see and feel things that others do not.

Up until the moment I became aware of this condition, I used to think that there was something very wrong with me. I spent most of my life living with the notion that I had a problem.

I am quite certain that I have had this ability all of my life but I never realized or utilized it until now, and as I sit here in the throes of soft middle age I can only hope that it is not too late to make something out of it — to make something out of my life.

These things that I profess to see and feel that others cannot are in plain sight. They are not hidden or exclusive to my senses (it is my belief that these things are simply overlooked or ignored by others). While other people tend to focus on the obvious, I live among the minutiae and the subtlety of life's main events. With some sort of built-in radar, I scan and notice the extreme details of what is happening around me.

To try to help make sense of this theoretical concept, I will provide concrete examples.

A portly, balding, middle-aged man drives past in a shiny new Ford Mustang convertible. The quick and easy reaction for most people would be to laugh and say, "Check out that guy and his midlife crisis car!" A short tempered mother is grocery shopping with her whining son and finally relents by giving him the candy he has been crying for. The natural thought for others is to think or say, "She spoils him. No wonder he is such a brat."

We all make assumptions and form opinions about what goes on around us. That is how the brain works - it is designed to take shortcuts, and it does not waste time trying to process and understand every detail. But sometimes our brain makes us more efficient at the expense of what is really happening. We fall into the trap of believing what we think we see - or what we want to see.

But for some reason I am a little different.

What could have been missed in the two examples are the details - that the man in the convertible also has a bumper sticker that reads, "One Day at a Time," and a license plate that spells, "THNKFL." Or that the woman with the screaming child has a prescription in one hand, fruits and vegetables among the pile of groceries, and is rubbing her forehead with her left hand - the ring finger void of any jewelry.

These minute details are seemingly irrelevant by themselves, but they can have a significant and illuminating effect on your point of view when pieced together. You might see the person you just observed in a different light. Seeing the bigger picture, the more detailed picture, can provide the observer with a better understanding, and can prevent the brain from making up its own ending to a person's story based on a small sampling of information.

Truth can be a relative thing and resisting the temptation to rush to judgment – or to judge at all – can change one's perspective. My Dad taught me that through his deeds and acts as a minister - that life is rarely black and white. A person's intentions and motivations cannot (should not) be presumed and summarized in a sentence or social media post.

It is my belief that I also have the ability to feel things about other people. I know this sounds either suspect or obvious, but what I mean to say is that I am hypersensitive to an individual's inner emotions. I can feel the goodness, hope, anger, kindness, sorrow, regret, love, pain, and hubris in people. There is an endless list of things that we as human beings can be, and whatever a person feels, I have the ability to feel it from within them...If I look into your eyes, I can see it and feel it from you:

I scan your body and clothes to see how they define you; I listen to what you say and live off your inflection and your cadence; I take in your blemishes and your beauty without discrimination; I interpret your posture and mannerisms and know where you are leading me; I accept your insecurities and confidence without questioning; I absorb you and all that makes you.

In my lifetime I have studied people from all walks of life and made their ticking minutes my own memories. I have observed neighbors and complete strangers and family and friends. I have watched people for short periods of time and followed them over a period of years. The more I follow and observe, the more of them I see and feel. The more I see and feel, the more embedded in my brain a person's experiences and emotions become - until I see their story and feel their story with my own senses.

This is not a condition that I turn on or off, and when it happens it is constant and quiet. I am wired this way.

While it may sound as if I am trying to portray this ability as some sort of gift or talent, please understand that is not the case. I have never been comfortable in my own skin. Up until this moment, I believed that seeing and feeling the lives of others was my affliction...

...When my family moved into my hometown in 1970, our arrival was printed in the local paper. We spent the next decade of my youth living among the people and places that I called home. But there came a time for us to leave, and when we did there was no public record or mention made, and I submit that the next chapter of my life (the one that should have been the most newsworthy) also went unwritten.

Something happened after I left my hometown. I lost my way. I became consumed and ensnared with living the lives of others, and by doing so I abandoned my own story. The pages that should have contained a productive and fulfilling personal narrative sat empty and yellowed with age, pegged with a lonely title as a placeholder: I am a Nothing Man.

When I left my hometown, I let slip the desire and the will to add content and substance to my own story. I allowed myself to be blown around by outside forces, and instead of moving forward and forging my own path, my mind remained anchored in the details, experiences, and landscape of my past. Therein lies my self-inflicted affliction, and it highlights the sad subplot of my own unwritten story: I moved away from my hometown, but I never moved on.

Life is not directed so that plot and storyline always make sense or come to a scripted conclusion - fairytale endings are best left for fairytales. In our real and imperfect lives, we characters struggle in our roles as heroes, villains, and passers-by. Sometimes, like me, we struggle to know what our role even is.

I remember my Dad telling me that as a young man he was "called" to seminary. There was an actual moment in time when he realized that ministering to the needs of others was what he wanted to do, and he quit his engineering job and took a path that led him in a very different direction. He changed course. Now is the time for me to take a page out of my Dad's book.

Something happens when we reach a certain age. There comes a time when we realize that we are running out of time - or at least feel as if we have wasted much of the time we have been given.

Our youth and our old-age serve as bookends, and everything that we do in between tells others our life story. We choose or discover a path and a purpose - as an artist, cook, store manager, teacher - whatever we do with our life propels us, and in the end, it defines us. As a middle-aged Nothing Man the window is closing on my time to become Something.

We humans are capable of many things, and our mark is made and legacy left through our relationships and our landscapes. These things reflect the level of care, abuse, or neglect that we provide them, and they grow and erode accordingly. The places we go and the people we know are our storytellers. But for the story of the human condition to be properly chronicled and shared somebody must be able to see the story, feel the story, and ultimately tell the story.

It is time for me to stop living the lives of others and time to tear off a fresh sheet of paper and begin writing my own story. I have come to realize that my affliction and my salvation are one in the same.

I have the mind of a writer, and my calling is to write about the lives of others.

ENDNOTES

[1] © 1997 Marian Chase, *Rowley, Massachusetts: An Historical Perspective*

[2] © 1997 Marian Chase, *Rowley, Massachusetts: An Historical Perspective*

Photos by Caroline Millin, except:

Learning to Fly '70 -Public Use, Flickr:
http://www.flickr.com/photos/30994245@N08/2898399430/

The Great Divide '75, Stock Image

A

B

Thank you to:

My wife, Debbie Millin for endless and honest edits, assurances, love, and support;

Caroline Millin for capturing words with images and for climbing to top of the bell tower with me;

Danny Millin for accepting my passion for writing despite despising the written word;

Paul and Betty Millin for practicing and teaching tolerance, conservation, and acceptance;

Benjamin Maxwell for sharing the rules of the English language - you taught me all I know about independent clauses, coordinating conjunctions, and use, of, the comma;

Jim "Webman" Connelly for pixilating me;

Chris Clarke for not asking if I printed this manuscript at work...several times;

Members of the 1st Congregational Church and the Town of Rowley, Massachusetts for allowing me to call your place home; and

Friends and family for seeing and supporting the writer in me.

Scott Millin
North Chelmsford, MA
www.scottmillin.com

C

D